The Parker Grey Show

The Parker Grey Show

KRISTEN BUCKLEY

BERKLEY BOOKS, NEW YORK

B

A Berkley Book
Published by The Berkley Publishing Group
A division of Penguin Group (USA) Inc.
375 Hudson Street
New York, New York 10014

This book is an original publication of The Berkley Publishing Group.

Copyright © 2003 by One Room Productions.
Cover illustration by Olaf Hajek.
Text design by Tiffany Kukec.

PRINTING HISTORY
Berkley trade paperback edition / July 2003

Library of Congress Cataloging-in-Publication Data

Buckley, Kristen.
The Parker Grey show / Kristen Buckley.
p. cm.
ISBN 0-425-19109-5 (pbk.)
1. Women detectives—New York (State)—New York—Fiction. 2. Manhattan
(New York, N.Y.)—Fiction. 3. Television viewers—Fiction. 4. Missing persons—
Fiction. 5. Young women—Fiction. 6. Waitresses—Fiction. I. Title.

PS3602.U35P37 2003
813'.6—dc21   2003048013

PRINTED IN THE UNITED STATES OF AMERICA

10 9 8 7 6 5 4 3 2 1

In memory of Raymond Bongiovanni

Love and thanks to:

Brian Regan
Howard Altman
Stephanie Staal
Amy Lipshutz
Ewan Leslie
Allison McCabe
Richard Pine
The Team at Endeavor
Joel McKuin
Kate Probst
Jennifer Harrington
And, of course, my little ones ...
Peyton & Liam

PROLOGUE

Lil's been kidnapped.

I know this because Smith just called to tell me. And Smith wouldn't lie. And now I have to go uptown to his office, where I'm sure he will have policemen and FBI and other sorts who handle this type of thing, but I can't find my keys. They're not where I left them, wherever the hell that might be. I'm tearing the place apart. Ripping through everything, as if the keys got up and walked away. I'm working myself up into a serious tizzy, and Humphrey's in the corner and it's pretty clear that he's enjoying this. But I'll deal with him later.

Because I've just spotted my keys.

Perched on the orange sofa. Right smack in the middle. I would have never put them there. Clearly the gods are conspiring against me. I grab the keys. Flip Humphrey the finger.

Which he deserves because, at this point, I'm convinced he's somehow involved. If not with Lil, then with the keys. As usual, Humphrey has no response. He just sits there like the big chunk of hollow wood that he is. Keys in hand, I leave the apartment. I've got a hot face, I haven't brushed my teeth, and I don't think it's even eight. On North Moore Street, I find myself cowering to avoid the sun. I've never been much of a morning person, and now I realize I forgot to lock the door. But at this point, with Lil being kidnapped, what are the odds of our apartment being robbed?

I blame this all on the plasma screen. Lil said doing bad things brings good karma, but we did a bad thing, and now it's nothing but bad dharma. And the cops, the FBI, they're going to ask me questions. And I'm going to have to lie. Which is fine. I'm adept at it. But what if they search the apartment? What if they find the screen? Then it's going to look fishy. Like I was somehow involved. Suddenly I'm a suspect. Suddenly I'm in jail for a crime I did not commit.

But I digress. I must not digress.

And so I change channels in my mind and think of M. The object of my obsession. The reason I get out of bed in the morning. And I couldn't even manage to say hello to him. All night I waited for Lil to come home, dying to tell her what happened. Dying to hear her spin. Dying for her to tell me that my sudden inability to speak was actually sexy or mysterious. Instead of pathetic, which is what it was. And now she's not here. She's been stolen. Taken. Kidnapped. Clearly, thinking about M is not going to help.

Just walk. One foot in front of the other.

I must keep it simple.

And so I head up North Moore, toward Hudson Street, because I stand a better chance of getting a cab. I should probably take a subway, but I think the occasion does not call for mass transit. My heart is pounding, and despite my best efforts, my mind is racing. My best friend has been *kidnapped*. Between the blistering morning sun and the giant scad of blue cheese hanging in the window of the gourmet shop on the corner, I have the unmistakable urge to vomit.

Lil is gone.

I think back to the last few days, to the utter insignificance of it all. She's out there, and I can't help her. I think about the sheer stupidity of life. About the fact that nothing ever makes sense and how we have no control over our destinies.

But mostly, I think about blue cheese.

ONE

It's Monday night, and I'm standing in front of some fat guy who's trying to decide whether he should have blue cheese or cheddar on his burger. I want to tell him he should have the salad, but I've only made fifty bucks, and I need a decent tip. I smile my benign waitress smile, as if I care, but the truth is all I'm thinking about is the tip. I have to get his check up to at least twenty bucks, or the tip is going to suck. If the tip sucks, I'll be forced to steal from the bar, and I really hate to do that because basically, deep down, I'm an honest person.

And he's taking forever to decide. Hedging. As if his response could mean life or death. I take a deep breath. Tell myself to relax. But breathing in the stench of stale beer and sawdust depresses me even more. So I go through the drill. I remind myself that working here is not so bad. The bar has a literary tradition. The entire Algonquin Round Table set spent many hours here, along with a certain Welsh poet who may or may not have drunk himself to death in our hallowed hall. Famous people come in all the time to drink and be seen. Although the only famous person I want to see is M. And he's yet to appear, despite the fact that he's mentioned his fondness for our establishment in several interviews. I know a lot about M. I know he likes to eat goat cheese and apples. I know he likes to sail. I know he had a dog that died of lymphoma whom he misses very much. But mostly, I know that I love M. Unfortunately, M doesn't know I exist.

And therein lies the rub.

I should probably move on, that would be the "healthy" thing to do, but as another famous person once said, "The heart wants what the heart wants." And even though my heart can't have M, the fact is, the mere thought of him fills me with an overwhelming sense of contentment. And suddenly, working at this smelly, decrepit bar doesn't seem so bad, although I still don't think this is what my mother had in mind for me when she used to say, "I'm raising you for greatness."

Whatever that means.

My mother sends me articles about young women my age. Covers from the *New York Times Magazine,* ads for Donna Karan featuring young, successful women. Interviews from *Mirabella.* All cut out with paper clips and little notes written in the margins like, "Thought you might find this interesting." Which loosely translated actually means, "This should be you." And maybe it should be me, but it isn't. Instead—

"You know what? Make it blue cheese."

Instead, it's blue cheese.

He snaps the menu back at me. I punch the order into a computer, words appear on the screen. I press Enter and they disappear. I walk back to the kitchen and wait by the printer, still in a brood. Still wondering how it has come to this. Of course I could blame the sadist I lived with for four years. I could blame it on our ugly breakup, which when I think about it, wasn't really very ugly at all. It was just swift. No, it wasn't the breakup. It was the four years that preceded it. It's the fact that I stayed. It's the fact that I allowed myself to wallow in such abject misery. The numeric code that is a hamburger with blue cheese reaches the printer and I translate for Pedro the fry cook: *"Hambergesa con queso azul."*

Pedro nods. Then he sticks out his tongue like a pervert.

Restaurant work is all about perversion and insults and killing time. I head back to my station. I put on my "I truly care" smile. Fat guy is getting another beer. "Let me get you another beer," I say. He looks up, another beer hadn't occurred to him, but with my smiling face, how can he say no?

"That'd be great."

The check is now at twenty-five dollars. I'm good for at least two bucks. Twenty more like him and I'll leave here with a hundred. I head to the bar to order the beer. I stand at the order station, but the bartender, John, is playing air guitar at the other end. Midway through the fifty-seventh chorus, he notices me.

"What can I get you, Parker?"

"Bass Ale."

He winks at me. Then pours.

I drop off the beer. Someone else has had mercy and dropped off the burger. I scan my section. I have no more customers. Looks like even the meager dream of making a hundred bucks is not in the cards tonight. To console myself, I grub a back rub off of Alden. He's an actor, very talented. I saw him in a play recently and was actually moved by his performance. He's all about acting for acting. He doesn't care about things like agents or head shots. He just likes to act; he likes the process. He pays the bills waiting tables. He says he's fulfilled. Sometimes I believe him. Sometimes I don't. But overall, he's an interesting guy and he gives an awesome shoulder rub. Waiting tables is also all about back rubs.

I have another hour to go. Another hour in my head. If I try hard enough, the reality of this melts away. And suddenly, it's just a play I'm in. One more act, and then I can go home. I look around as Alden works my knots. It's the usual cast of characters. The quiet guy who eats alone reading a sports page. All the middle-aged guys who sit at the bar and don't talk. And, of course, the girls. There are a few tonight. Not as many as on a weekend, but they're still here. All tarted up, looking for action. By the end of the night, they're falling all over me, drunk and sloppy with their big raccoon eyes, begging me for water. The blue cheese guy wants his check. My shoulder rub is brought to an abrupt halt and I bring it over. I drop it on the table and thank him with a big smile.

"Are you an actor?"

It's a loaded question, because we're all, to a certain degree, actors. We all wear masks to hide who we really are. At least, that's what I've always thought. I size him up quickly. He's terribly overweight, he has poor dietary habits, and he's reading the *Post*. I choose the profession that I believe will impress him the most. I do this because, more than anything, I don't want him to think I'm a girl with a dream who's down on her luck. "Actually, I'm in med school."

Med school. Not only do I have brains, but I'm busting my hump waiting tables to pay my own way. No free rides here.

"Fordham?"

"No, Columbia." Fordham is for losers. He looks really impressed. This pleases me.

"What kind of medicine are you looking to go into?"

"Actually, I want to go into research."

"You'll never make money doing that."

Everyone's an expert. Who's to say that I won't become a celebrated researcher? Perhaps I'm the one who discovers the cure for cancer. In my lies, I'm always successful. "It's not about money."

He gets up and leaves me a five, which surprises me. He had deuce written all over him. "It's always about money. Don't kid yourself."

I take the five off the table and clear away his dirty plate. I suppose he's right. It is all about money. But I never seem to have much of it and I can't envision a time when things will be any different. At this point in my life, although I try not to think about it, I don't know what I want to do or who I want to be anymore. The truth is, since I quit playing, I'm completely lost and if I think about what's going to become of me, I freak out. In a moment of weakness I confided this to my mother. Her response was to send me an article about 401(k)s. I think about that article and laugh as I scrape the plate off and toss it into a bin for washing.

"Parker, you seem out of it. Why don't you head home? It's dead."

I turn and see Alden. "You think? What if Tommy comes?" Tommy is our raging alcoholic boss, who only last week tried to strangle his brother-in-law at a barbecue.

"He called earlier, said someone could go if it was slow."

"Thanks, Alden." Before I go, when no one's looking, I skim twenty bucks off of a beer tab. As I pocket the money, I pray to all gods of all religions simultaneously for forgiveness.

TWO

Thankfully, my living arrangements are amazing. If they weren't, things would be far bleaker than they already are. But as Lil says, square footage is a mood elevator. And with four thousand square feet, thirty-foot ceilings, eastern and western exposures, walls of glass, an enormous kitchen with a great island, an immense window seat that spans the width of the apartment, white oak floors, hulking beams, two enclosed bedrooms, and lots of recessed lighting, how depressed can you get? The only thing missing from our lives is living room furniture; the one piece we have is a hideous orange velvet sectional that Lil found at a flea market. Lil argues that our lack of furniture only serves to make the place look bigger. And in Manhattan, bigger is always better.

I moved in with Lil after I left Dana. I had nowhere to go,

and so I ended up on her doorstep with all my crap, like some postmodern Felix Unger. She opened the door, took one look at me, and summed it all up in her own Lil way: "Never trust a guy with a girl's name." That's all she said, then she opened the door and I moved in. It was that simple. That's how it is with Lil and me. Simple but complicated. Simple in that we know each other completely. Complicated for the same reason. The greatest part of the whole setup is there's no rent. Lil's father owns the building. Back before the boom years, before rogue traders jacked up all the prices, he had a vision. He thought Tribeca would be something when no one else did. He bought up buildings, and now he owns ten down here, and in SoHo and Chelsea. He leases them out for a fortune, but he lets Lil live for free.

With my stolen twenty dollars still causing me guilt, I get home and I can hear right away that Stockbroker Guy, our neighbor down below, has once again fallen asleep with the TV on. The noise is blaring through the vents. Ricocheting off of the support beams. Our floor is literally throbbing. And Lil is pissed. She's standing by the kitchen island, decked out in an Elvis costume, from his bloated period, complete with rhinestone pants, white cape, sideburns, and glasses. I laugh, and Lil gives me a dirty look. Lil takes Elvis very seriously. Elvis as the cultural icon, Elvis as the purveyor of the American Dream that in the end, even he couldn't live inside. "It's called common courtesy!" she shouts. "The guy thinks he's the fucking king of the universe! With his town cars and his million-dollar bonuses!"

I shout, "What's with the Elvis clothes?!" not sure if she hears me.

Telephone in hand, she keeps hitting speed dial to get his apartment. "The Viva Las Vegas Sing-Along at Symphony Space," she hollers back, gesturing with her hand as if I'm supposed to understand the rest. The giant studded glasses are slipping down her nose. She looks at me, those Betty Boop eyes of hers bulging at the retinas. "You *know* he's just got it off the hook! Can you believe his entitlement? !" She slams the phone down. Glares at the boxes of paper piled along the southern wall. "Parker, what's the deal with this paper? Are we going into the copy business?"

"That's prime origami-grade paper."

"Yeah, you've told me, but there are twenty-seven boxes of it, and it's been sitting here for a month!" She snatches the phone back up, about to blow.

During a frantic afternoon spent looking up information on textile design—which I considered pursuing as a career until I realized that my only qualification was owning a large collection of Dorothy Liebes fabrics—I came across a fascinating article about a small group of Japanese monks who practiced origami. They found meaning in the folding of paper. The act itself consumed them for hours each day and led to periods of intense enlightenment. Amazing stuff. Later, I walked home and passed a man on the street selling a bulk load of prime-grade origami paper. I considered it a sign and bought all twenty-seven boxes for two hundred dollars. But that was a month ago, and I still haven't started folding. "Don't get all pissy at *me* just because Stockbroker Guy is blasting his TV."

Lil backs off but continues to speed dial, even though we both know it's futile. "Oh, yeah, your spiritual advisor called and left some rambling message. Does the word *brevity* mean anything to that girl?"

Now she's speaking about Trudy, who I met through work. Trudy's very into therapy and seems to have a vested interest in fixing my life, which suits me just fine, because at this point, I can use all the help I can get. "Trudy's okay. She's just very talky—"

"Annoying is more like it. And has she done anything about that unibrow?"

"I don't know; I haven't seen her in a while." I grab a bottled water out of the fridge, turning my back and hopefully ending this conversation. Then I look over at Humphrey. He's been out for months and I haven't touched him. I can't bring myself to touch him. I want him to go away. I want to yank off those six strings and burn his body for kindling. I can feel Lil watching me. I'm aware of the fact that she knows exactly what I'm thinking, and if I try to harm Humphrey in any way, she'll stop me. Humphrey knows this too. Lil's convinced I'm working through something. She says I have the musical equivalent of writer's block, and that I need to stare it down. I don't want to believe she's right. I can't go back to living the way I did, and I don't know any other alternatives. I run my hands under hot water; the muscles ache from atrophy. I went from playing six hours a day to nothing. Larry King is booming from down below.

"*Hello Sioux City. . . .*"

"*Yeah, hi, Larry. . . .*"

"Who are these people calling in from all over the country? I would never *dream* of calling in to a show. Would you?" This is her way of apologizing for pissiness.

I shake my head no. Not in a million years.

"We're going down. We've gotta confront him."

I cringe. I hate confrontation. Lil knows this.

"Relax. I'll do the confronting. You can just, you know, stand next to me."

We head down together. We get to his door, 3H. We knock, and the door pushes open. It's all very mysterious.

"Holy shit, he's dead!"

"He's not *dead*, Parker."

Lil has no way of knowing that for sure, and I suspect deep down, she'd think it was cool if he were. We go in and find Stockbroker Guy passed out on a giant, black leather recliner. Lil waves her hand in front of his face. Nothing.

"You sure he's not dead?"

"Dead people don't snore."

I can't help but look at him with disdain. Sitting there in his suit, his fly undone, snoring. It shows a general lack of respect for himself and, quite frankly, for the suit, which, I notice, is a fine Italian silk wool blend. We have a look around. It's always interesting to see the way other people live. It's clear he has a lot of money, yet the overusage of black leather is a plain indication that he's got no taste. Apparently, there's a girl in the picture, although from her photo, it seems she lives in some sort of tropical climate and isn't around often. Lil points out that judging from the take-out containers and the lack of silverware, she isn't around *ever*. Then there are his windows, which are covered with water stains and bird crap.

"Why bother living in a loft if you're not going to have clean windows?" Lil asks, and I shrug my shoulders in agreement. Lil is fanatical about keeping our windows clean. Her father pays a guy to come once a month. "Why my father ever rented to this a-hole is a mystery to me. He should do more in the screening process."

She heads over to the giant plasma screen that is the TV. I've read about these things, seen them in magazines but never up close. My initial reaction is that Larry King on a giant screen is a bad thing.

"Hello, Detroit?"

"Ah, yeah hi, Larry. . . . I really hate these people who think they can come in . . ."

We can't figure out where the knobs are. The thing is built into the wall. It's all very techno, like something out of *The Jetsons*. Finally, we find the remote. After a few seconds, we figure out how to lower the sound. Then we change the channel, surfing until we hit a music video. And we both just stop.

"Look at the definition!"

"The color saturation is tremendous!"

I can't take my eyes off it. Neither can Lil. How can we ever go back to our crappy Panasonic? I look at her. I know what she's thinking. "We can't."

"Why can't we?"

"It's theft."

"It isn't theft. It's redistribution." Lil would make a good socialist.

I'll admit, I want the screen. I want the colors. If I could climb into it, I would; it's like a Rothko painting. The colors humming with a womblike precision. Stockbroker Guy stirs. We run around like chickens with our heads cut off and dive behind the monolith black leather sofa. He belts out a loud fart.

And the fate of the plasma screen is sealed.

We run upstairs for tools. Lil in her Elvis getup, rifling through drawers, and me standing there, tentative, the hot twenty now burning a hole in my pocket. "I don't know, Lil. I've got mixed feelings." She ignores me. "My life isn't exactly coming up roses, and I don't want to make things worse."

Lil stops and looks at me, like she's looked at me a thousand times before, wondering why the hell it's always the same conversation. "There's nothing wrong with doing bad things," she finally says. "Doing bad things is a part of human nature, and when you do bad things, you release negative energy, which counteracts with positive energy. The negative ions go out, and positive ions come back in their place." She takes the stairs two at a time and mutters over her shoulder, "This is why the rich get richer."

★

Back in Stockbroker Guy's apartment, with the only two tools we own in hand, a Phillips-head screwdriver and a needle-nose pliers, I stare at the screen. I'm still a little concerned about the karmic repercussions. But the color is so beautiful. I'm certain Stockbroker Guy doesn't appreciate it. The screen deserves better. I decide that Lil is right. I'm going to do a bad thing, and hopefully something good will come back to me. It takes us forty minutes to get the screen off the wall. And all the while he's just sitting there sleeping. We pile the wires, which spill out of the wall like guts, onto the screen and carry it upstairs. We lay it on the orange sofa and collapse on the floor. Exhausted. We get our story straight. We were both out. I was at work, and Lil was at the Symphony Space sing-along. The Elvis costume will serve as evidence. We have no idea what happened. We'll let it blow over for a few days, and then we'll install it. We hide it in Lil's room, and when we're done, she collapses on her bed, which is covered with books. I pull off her white leather boots and leave her to her exhaustion.

The apartment is so still. I like it this way. I shut out the lights and head over to the island. I pull a cigarette out of the box, light it out of habit more than anything else. I see my videotapes on the counter; I grab the one on the top and stick it into our crappy Panasonic. The smoke swirls around my head, drips down my throat. I exhale, and my show starts. *MEDS*, your basic soap opera set in a hospital. M is on the show; he plays a doctor from war-torn Croatia, which is really where he is from. They brought him in two and a half seasons ago to replace some idiot who thought he was going to have a film career. Now that guy is nowhere, and M is the star of the show. I've got the entire season on tape, every M moment at my disposal. It's the only thing getting me through their hiatus.

I fast-forward past the credits, until M comes on the screen. He's helping a pregnant teen. I toss the cigarette into the sink. I'm too tired to smoke. I peel off my clothes, down to my underwear. Then I grab the set and drag it up into the window seat, wrapping a blanket around myself as a buffer from the glassy chill coming off the window. I lie down, M at my feet. His dark eyes, his deep voice. His amazing accent. I touch the screen with my foot, covering up the girl, so there is only him and me.

"How can I help you?"

Just keep me company.

"I'm here for you."

Stay with me while I sleep.

"You can't keep on living like this."

I know, but I don't want to talk about it now.

I feel myself slipping, and the more I surrender to it, the more real it all is. Like he's right next to me, talking to me. I struggle to keep my mind awake, but I'm melting out of myself. And all at once I'm on a boat, it's the two of us, and I'm about to kiss him, but the waves come. Choppy at first and then violent and I'm still trying to kiss him, but I fall. I fall down the slippery deck, heading for the water. I think he's going to catch me. I think he's going to reach a hand out. But he's sitting at the top of the boat. He's fine, and I'm plunging into the water. I dart up, my leg does a weird kick, a reflex motion, and then I hear his voice and bolt straight up.

My mouth is dry, my heart is pounding.

It's always the same dream. Me falling into the water, but tonight M's voice woke me. I look and see him on the screen. I swear he's looking at me. Those dreamy brown eyes of his. I'm flooded with the certainty that I can see behind those eyes, and that I know him. My jaw hurts. It's throbbing. It has been for weeks. I need to see a dentist, but I don't have health insurance. I could go to a clinic, but the use of the words *dentist* and *clinic* together scares me. God, I need water. And M is still looking at me, and I want to run to a mirror, because my thirst is so great I'm certain that I've got raccoon eyes like those tarts at the bar. And now I can't find M. He's gone, but he's trying to call me, and I can't find the phone. I'm running around, looking all over the apartment, the street, the Chinese restaurant on Tenth Street. But there's no phone. And yet I can hear it ring. I know it's there. And there's a terrible grinding noise.

Which is the big clue.

This is still a dream, and I'm grinding my teeth down to a pulp.

I sit up. My jaw throbbing, the tape over, nothing but snow. It all seemed so real. I look at the clock. I've been asleep for an hour. And the phone is ringing. I know it's not for me. No one ever calls me. Well, no one besides Trudy and my mother. But not at this hour. It's Lil's boyfriend, Mr. Smith. Of that much I can be sure. I assume it's been ringing for at least twenty minutes. She likes to make him wait, and Mr. Smith always waits. Mr. Smith is not his real name. We started calling him that because he is an extremely well-known mogul. Lil felt that it would make it easier for us to talk about him when we're in public. He's too well known for us to just blurt out his name and talk about things like how his wife has him by the balls. Why his wife has put up with his infidelities for forty years is beyond me. Lil says a billion dollars and you'd put up with anything. But I'm not so sure. I have a low tolerance when it comes to betrayal. But that's just me.

The phone has now rung twenty times. Anyone else would have hung up, but for Mr. Smith, it's pathological. All day long everyone kisses his ass, doors open when he enters a room, people do whatever he wants. The only one in the world who reminds him that his shit stinks is Lil. She's brutal. Last Christmas he came bearing gifts, but he was late. He kept her from getting to her father's on time, which was no great loss, since Christmas with Lil's father usually involves sitting around a table screaming. Back in the day, her father was a raging alcoholic. He used to put her on top of the china breakfront in the dining room and tell her to jump. She, of course, would be crying and terrified. Her parents divorced, and the breakfront diving came to a halt, but the damage was done. Lil will never forgive him. He tried to make amends when he sobered up, but it was already too late then. And now they're still caught up in the dance of it, and he's paying in square footage, among other things.

Anyway, Lil's point, and she had one, was that no one keeps Mr. Smith waiting, so who the hell did he think he was that he could keep her waiting? She ended up kicking his gifts down the stairs, punting them one at a time. The look on his face was priceless. He sulked off, and the next day, twice as many presents were delivered, all from Neiman Marcus and Tiffany. Lil felt that her point was well taken.

The thing I find most disturbing about the relationship is that Mr. Smith is seventy-five years old. I can't believe she's sleeping with a septuagenarian. I've seen old-man ass and it's not pretty.

The phone is still ringing. I decide to break the dysfunction and answer it.

"Hello?"

"Yes, Lil please."

He's always very polite to me.

"One moment."

I go into her room and find her reading some esoteric thing about finance and its effect on art commerce in China. Lil is brilliant, completely brilliant, which is why, I've often thought, she needs to occupy herself with nonsense.

"You shouldn't have picked up. I was going for a hundred rings."

"What's the record?"

She licks a finger and turns a page. "Seventy."

"I didn't know. I won't answer next time."

She takes the phone. The conversation is very brief.

"What. I'm reading. Nothing you'd understand."

Lil flaunts her intelligence like a supermodel flaunts her beauty. I like that about her. I admire it. She doesn't brag, she just blows you away. She has four degrees, two of them master's, and now she's in law school. One day her head is going to reach peak capacity. I have visions of it exploding all over North Moore Street. She hangs up the phone.

"Smith is coming over."

"Ugh."

"I know, sorry. But he wants sex, and it's not like we can go to a hotel."

"Why don't you go to his place?"

" 'Cause his *wife's* there."

Lil's getting testy with me. It bugs her that I find her sex life with Smith to be, for lack of a better word, repulsive. And so I put the phone back on the receiver, pull on my headphones, and insert the two-hour season finale of *MEDS* into the machine. With any luck, I'll fall asleep before Smith arrives.

★

The door slams shut, startling me awake. The headphones from last night are coiled around my neck like a noose. I open my eyes and see it's already morning. The sun's streaming in the window, I curl up my legs, trying to hide from its reach. I grab a cigarette from my pack. My teeth are coated in a horrific film, and my jaw is aching, but I light up, and the warm smoke feels good going down my throat. I look over and see that it's almost eight. I haven't been up this early in months. I consider going back to sleep, and then I think of Caroline. I haven't seen her in ages. If I hurry, I can make it.

I pull on my stinky bar clothes from last night, brush my teeth, and give myself an all-over body shot with a can of Right Guard. Then I head out to the small bodega on the corner of Eleventh and Washington. They make the best egg sandwiches. They also have cute kittens. Apparently they haven't heard about the concept of neutering, so there's always a new litter meowing around. But the egg sandwiches are sublime.

I head in.

THREE

And sure enough, there's Caroline. Caroline's a book scout. I have visions of her creeping around the city with a giant magnifying glass. I see her trolling rivers and culling through garbage dumps, like some bibliophile explorer hunting the wilderness in search of the written word. We met at this very bodega, over egg sandwiches, kittens, and smokes, which we'd sit on the stoop sharing until she had to go to work and I had to go back home to do my morning practice. That was back when I was still playing guitar and I lived with Dana on Eleventh Street. Caroline and I have a few key things in common, and no matter how much time passes, there's never a need to fill in the blanks.

"You wan' cheese on that?"

"No. Just the eggs . . ." Caroline is clearly down; she hasn't ordered cheese on her sandwich, which she usually does. I sidle up to her. "Egg sandwich, cheese, bacon, and put some cheese on hers too. She wants it, she just doesn't think she does."

Caroline turns, sees me, and smiles a small, sad smile. And then I remember the blurb in the *Post*. They've canceled *La Femme Nikita*. She's in mourning. I've always been partial to the movie, but for Caroline, it was all about the series. I offer my condolences and ask, "How are you holding up?"

"I'm just so upset." She sighs. "I see Nikita stuck there in operations, saving the world, and I don't understand why Michael left her. I *know* he had to take care of his son, but couldn't they *just get a nanny?* Couldn't they have worked something out?" Now she's speaking very rapidly. "I can't *believe* this is how it's all ended. *Five* years!" Her voice rises to an unusual pitch. "I've lived for Sunday nights, and at the very least I figured *they'd give me a happy ending!*"

The guy behind the counter looks like he's ready to toss both of us out. I must calm her down; I'm not leaving without my egg sandwich. Thankfully, I have a working knowledge of the show. I tell her in a soothing voice that Michael will come back and visit. He loves Nikita, and I'm certain that despite the maudlin ending, the implication that they'd never be together again, he will return because he loves her.

Caroline smiles. "Do you think?"

"Yeah. You know Michael. He's not gonna leave her all alone."

We get our sandwiches and head outside to the stoop.

"How's M?"

Caroline is one of the few people who know how I feel about M. But still, I don't think she fully understands the extent of my feelings. I haven't gone into too much detail. It's enough that she accepts my obsession. "He's okay. Although I couldn't believe the season finale. That nurse dumped him for the other resident."

"What a cunt."

"And now they're on hiatus, so basically, it's rerun central."

"If Nikita was a repeat, I'd just want to shove a machete through the set."

We alternate bites of warm egg with drags on a cigarette that we're sharing. "So, what else is going on?"

"Not much. I'm just depressed. What about you? How's your music?"

I realize that I haven't seen Caroline in nearly six months. And this is a topic I really don't want to get into in any great detail. "I quit."

"What?"

She looks genuinely shocked. I wonder why. It's not like *she* quit.

"No! I don't believe it!"

But I assure her that I've quit, much to the chagrin of my entire family, who are all worried about me. All except for my mother, who's just pissed. She raised me for greatness, and I went and quit. It's not sitting well with her. She tells my older sister that she fears for my future. Then she sends me articles. I try to avoid her calls now, because she always sounds so panicked: *"What are you going to do?" "What about money?"*

"How long can you live with Lil?" She wants answers, and I have none. I feel myself getting stressed. The hot face, the dry mouth, the pain in my stomach . . .

"You haven't quit, Parker. You're just on hiatus, like M."

Something about the way she says it makes everything seem okay. And this is why I love Caroline. She takes a drag of her cigarette. Then she smiles. Caroline has a great smile. I often wish it were mine. Then she looks at her watch and sighs.

"I hate my job. I wish I could go work for Nikita."

"Figure out a way, and I'd join you in a heartbeat."

Caroline laughs just a little. "You think everyone's as weird as us?"

It's an interesting question. I consider it briefly and then respond. "We're like the ambassadors of Weird, only they moved the embassy and won't tell us where it is." I'm joking, but Caroline takes it to heart.

"That's sort of poetic."

"You think?"

She laughs. "In a weird way, yeah." She gets up, snuffs out the smoke with her shoe. "It's fucked-up, Parker. They canceled a show. A friggin' show, and I'm all bent outta shape."

"Just go with it. What're you gonna do? You can't help the way you feel."

She nods, looks down, thinking. "I used to think that it was all about Michael. I just wanted that kind of burning love, you know, shrouded in excellent clothes and exotic locales. But now that it's all over . . . Now I think I just wanted to be Nikita. I just want to be her. She's out there somewhere, keeping the world safe for people like you and me. And what do I do? I scout books for foreign publishers." She lights another cigarette and takes a deep, contemplative drag. "That's my big contribution. I go to parties, and people are chatting about ridiculous bullshit, and I could give a crap. It used to be that I could pass the time thinking of Michael and Nikita. Now there's nothing." Caroline snuffs out her cigarette. "This is my life. It's not what I expected."

FOUR

As I walk home, I take solace in knowing that I'm not the only one who feels completely adrift. I open the door to the apartment, and Lil's in her bathrobe yelling at three beefy Russian guys who work for her father. Someone once told me that the Russian mob has a monopoly on roasted nut carts throughout the city. I don't know why I think of this.

"I'm glad you're here!" Lil waves me over. "You've got a better visual sense than me. Where should we put this thing?" The three guys are all sweaty, holding the plasma screen up to different walls for her approval.

"Are you sure this is okay?"

"Totally kosher. Cops were here this morning. Took a report and split. Then Stockbroker Guy admitted to leaving his door open, so all bets are off."

Who knew grand larceny could be so easy? I walk around the apartment, searching for the perfect spot for our new fifteen thousand–dollar TV. When I stand by the window seat, it becomes instantly clear: It must go on the giant support beam in front of the kitchen island. I point to the spot.

"Facing *outside*? Wouldn't it be better if we put it on the other side, so we can watch from the couch?"

"No, it's good. This way we can watch when we're in the kitchen *and* when we're on the window seat." The best part of this apartment is the window seat. The Russians are muttering to themselves. They put up with Lil to keep her father happy, but it's clear they're annoyed. A decision has to be made. I point to the beam. They get to work before Lil has a chance to argue. Then I sense disapproval, but I don't think it's coming from them. They have no problem with items that fall off the proverbial back of the truck. No, it's not them. I look over at Humphrey, perched in his stand, in his usual spot in the corner.

It's Humphrey that doesn't approve.

I give him the finger and turn my back.

Lil joins me over at the island. We watch the Russians as they dig into the beam, breaking through the wallboard. The plaster falling onto the floor, the wiring shoved into the cavity. It's all very clinical. The DVD player, the VCR added into the wall, like a bowel obstruction caught halfway through the operation. When they finish, we stare at the monolith hanging on our beam. A veritable shrine to the moving picture. I turn it on. It hums for a moment before the picture comes into frame. We're quiet, as if in the presence of something greater than ourselves. It's like a religious icon. I whisper this to Lil, and she launches into a short tirade about the advent of television and the subsequent demise of Western civilization, and how this in turn impacted the economic growth of countries like Brazil. I'm not listening, and the Russians are all making a mad dash for the door before Lil drags the fall of the Soviet empire into her economic diatribe. The picture comes up; it's an old movie in Technicolor with hoards of men in sailor suits, dancing around singing.

I wish I lived in a world where spontaneous dance numbers were the norm.

Next to me Lil's still off on a tangent. Every few moments I nod my head, but I'm not hearing a word. I'm too busy staring at the screen. I'm in awe of it. Mesmerized by the color saturation. Without thinking, I grab a pen off the counter. A smelly sharpie, I don't know where it came from. It must be Lil's. I walk under the screen and write a sentence. Nothing brilliant, just a group of words that traveled from my brain to the wall in a strange cursive script that is not my own. It's an act without premeditation. Without intent.

"Parker? What are you *doing?!*"

And before I can send the message from my brain to my hand to stop writing, the sentence is complete. On the wall, just under the screen, in big letters: "AND SO IT BEGINS." Lil takes the pen out of my hand. "Parker, you're writing on the wall?" She is staring at me wide-eyed, as if waiting for an explanation.

I don't know why I did it.

I laugh. There's something so ridiculous about it. I'm writing on the walls, like a child! And yet something about it felt so liberating. Naughty, maybe. I think of Bonnie Cashin, the famed designer who invented the Coach bag among other things. I read about her in an article my mother sent. Bonnie Cashin had a graffiti wall. It was immense, I saw photos of it, all these words scrawled on a plain white wall. She said she liked to surround herself with color and words. She said it filled her with glee. And glee is something that I am very much in need of.

Lil grabs her stuff and tells me she is leaving for a seminar on torts. She mutes the TV and makes me promise that I won't write on the walls anymore. I agree to the promise, at least in theory. Then the door slams, and the apartment is silent.

Normally, if normal could describe the last decade of my life, I'd grab Humphrey and get to work. Practicing scales, arpeggios, and some simple etudes to warm up my hands. And then I'd spend five hours working on a piece or two. Bach, Vivaldi, sometimes obscure Italian pieces. Hours spent trying to train my fingers to make a run or to turn a phrase. And then night would come. And I'd eat and spend the rest of the night listening to everything and anything I could get my hands on. Until I fell asleep. Then I'd get up and do it all over again.

But not anymore.

FIVE

As far back as I can remember, my life was regimented, the hours doled out for different parts of my musical training. I did not go to proms; I did not hang out after school. I did not do any of those things despite the fact that my mother, my friends, my family all begged me to. For some reason I felt the need for self-imposed exile early on. Trudy, my expert in all things psychological, says it has to do with my parents' divorce. That it was all some way to bury my emotions or not focus on myself. But I can't say for sure that that's why I did it. I can't say for sure why I've done anything. All I know is that now I marvel over things like sitting in the park at three in the afternoon on a Saturday. I was always in school on Saturday. Composition, harmony, theory—there was always something new to learn. There was always another piece to listen to, another composer to understand, another song to dissect.

Always something to keep me from life.

But all that is behind me now, and I can do things that I've never done. When I'm not panicking, sometimes I'm truly amazed at the freedom I feel. I'm still faced with the nagging question: Why did I live like that for ten years? To sit in a room alone and play someone else's songs? To spend a year on a piece for a performance in a stodgy concert hall where most of the people would struggle to stay awake? And I don't have an answer. I don't know. I only know that I can't do it anymore. But now I have my plasma screen, and I have color, and I have a sentence on the wall that feels like the purest form of self-expression ever to come out of me. Right now, all I want to do is watch movies. I want to see color up on my plasma shrine.

★

I have promised Lil that I won't partake in any further wall writing, but I'm not so sure that I can keep it. I feel compelled to do it again. Like a turretic who can't stop cursing. Even as I schlep all the way to Kim's on Bleecker Street because I like their video selection, I can think of things I want to write. I see the words in my mind, forming a line. I try to ignore them as I browse, looking for *The Last Emperor* and *Ju Dou*. Both of these movies are all about color. For whatever reason, I'm craving color. I will not write, I reason with myself, but I *will* watch color. I search Kim's for about twenty minutes but can't find either movie. Finally, I ask the girl at the counter.

"I'm looking for *The Last Emperor,* and I can't seem to find it." She looks at me like I'm a turd she nearly stepped in. I struggle on. "I searched historical epics and Bertolucci, but I'm not seeing it. . . ."

She pauses, a long pause. I am wasting her time. The kids at Kim's are a very cruel and surly bunch. Yet I'm a customer, so she is compelled to answer.

"*Last Emperor* is in costume design," she says in a voice reserved for morons.

Costume design. Of *course.* I'm about to be pissed, but then I think of Bonnie Cashin. She was a costume designer. I wonder if perhaps it's a sign. As I mull it over, counter girl moves on. It seems there's a one-question limit at Kim's, so I go back and begin an exhaustive search for *Ju Dou.* Foreign Directors, Production Design, Chinese Art Films, Cinematography, Movies About Peasants . . . Finally, I find it under Cannes Winners. I leave with the films, thinking about Bonnie Cashin and my graffiti wall. The words in my head are shouting now. They want to get out. They want off the bus. I tell them to sit their asses back down, but I head for Pearl Paints, the Mecca of art supply stores on Canal Street, anyway.

★

Pearl Paints. Since I was a kid, and my mother would take me there, I've felt drawn to it. As if the elusive keys to my happiness are somehow hidden in the store. If only I could find the right art supply, the door will open. Somehow, something will give, and my life will be imbued with a deeper meaning.

So far it hasn't happened, but still I keep returning. Buying things I don't need. Boxes of pencils, watercolor sets, high-grade drawing paper. None of it has ever seen the light of day.

I spend two hours just looking around. Then I drop a hundred bucks on pens. Various shapes, grades, thicknesses, and colors. I even buy inkpots and brushes. I tell myself that I have to have them. Origami monks, Bonnie Cashin, *The Last Emperor*. Words. Color. Ink. Somehow it's all tied into the same thing. The swirl, the vortex, of who I am. It's nearly dark when I get home. It's amazing how you can waste a day. The time just goes. Lil is still at school; she won't be home until late. I cook myself an omelet. Then I put in *Last Emperor*, but I don't bother with the sound.

I only want the picture.

A music teacher once made me watch movies without sound in order to learn structure. She said when I understood structure, I would understand Bach, and if I understood Bach, I would understand everything there was to know about life. Music teachers love to say things like this, but it's only a ruse designed to confuse their students so that they'll grow frustrated and eventually quit.

I stare at the screen. John Lone is trying to slit his wrists. The blood in the sink moves from sepia to deep red, and we're transported back to his boyhood. To the Forbidden City, where the blood of death is now the vibrant blood of life. It's warm. I pull off my pants and shirt. I'm in my bra and underwear; the windows have no coverings, but I couldn't care less. I reach for one of my new pens. A thick one, red. Permanent. Lil's going to kill me.

But I have no choice.

I climb onto the island, stepping into the sink, the cold metal against my feet, and then over to the far edge. Just in front of the beam that holds the plasma screen, and I lean over. My arm braced against the top of the beam, my toes clinging to the edge of the island. John Lone has his head in my belly. I take the red marker and write without thought. Just one word after another in the white space just above the screen. This continues. Me, the movie, the pens, the smell of ink. Slowly spelling out words as they exit my mind and jump onto the wall. I don't know what I'm doing. But it feels right, and nothing's felt right for a very long time.

"I knew if I left you alone, you'd do something like this." Lil is home.

Busted. In my underwear, a smoke dangling out of my mouth. Hanging off the island, my palm clinging to the beam the only thing keeping me from me hitting the floor. Lil drops her keys and picks at a few pieces of egg that stuck to the pan. I look at her from under my arm. Waiting to see if there's going to be more. But there isn't. She looks up at the screen.

"That John Lone is a serious piece of ass."

That's all she says, and then she goes to bed. And I know that somehow, in her silence, there is approval.

SIX

I can't move my mouth. At least, not without pain. Lil makes tea as I sit crosslegged on the island holding my jaw. I look at the clock and groan; I have to go to work in an hour. "This is ridiculous." She puts the teapot down. "Stop groaning. You're going to the dentist. Today. Put it on a credit card."

I call work. The pain is so bad I don't even care about incurring more debt. I switch my shift with a girl named Rio. Lil and I take three trains to get to her father's dentist. My jaw is throbbing the whole way. Lil says it's all internalized stress. I don't argue with her; I just want the pain to stop. My hands are covered with ink from the permanent markers I've been using, a clear indication that the wall writing could potentially spiral out of control. Lil glances at them and says casually, "You might want to consider a journal. At the rate you're going, we're going to run out of wall space."

★

I'm ushered into a chair at once. Lil said the dentist saved her father's teeth. She told me this as if his teeth had cancer. But in fact, they were just terribly yellowed. Her father is very proud of his teeth, now that they have been bleached back to glory. The hygienist comes in. She gives me the once-over, and I know in a moment that she knows I haven't been flossing regularly. She slides up in her chair, snaps on her gloves.

"Let's have a look, shall we?"

She makes a few sounds as she pokes around with a sharp metal object. I'm nervous. Uptight. And she's enjoying it. It's the hygienist power trip.

"A young girl like yourself, you really need to floss."

She's got her hands in my mouth, so I can only nod and grunt, "Uh-huh."

"You probably want to get married and have children at some point, but with these gums, you're never going to find anyone."

I don't know how to respond. I'm appalled that she can make this type of judgmental remark. This is a woman who, after all, spends her day scraping crap off other people's teeth! I'm livid, but my jaw is aching, so I grunt nothing. She leaves, and the dentist comes in with a smile. Like good cop, bad cop. The dentist sits down, pulls on rubber gloves, and then covers her nose and mouth.

"Let's have a look."

I can barely open up. She sticks her fingers in my mouth.

Has me bite down a few times, then she messes with my jaw and nods. "TMJ. Temporomandibular joint syndrome. You'll need to wear a brace at night when you sleep."

I have visions of headgear. "For how long?"

She smiles at me. "Forever."

It could be worse. I could have a colostomy bag.

"We're going to take some impressions, and you'll come back in ten days for your fitting."

Ten days? I can't open my mouth! But she's one step ahead of me. "In the meantime I'm going to give you some Percocet to ease the pain."

Percocet? No, no. Those are strong. "I don't want that. It's too strong."

"Just take them as prescribed, and you'll be fine."

I lived with a pill popper for four years, and I've no intention of becoming all messed up like he was. You read about these people strung out on prescription painkillers, and you think nothing of it. It almost sounds glamorous, until you live with one of them and your life becomes a living hell. I'm not going to end up like some character from the *Days of Wine and Roses*. Sitting at a window pining away for an elusive high. Trapped in a never-ending cycle of recovery. Taking inventories, making amends, working the program. Screw that. I'd rather live with the pain.

I sit in the chair for a few minutes while they put giant mouth-pieces filled with goo that feels like silly putty into my mouth. It's all very uncomfortable. The only upside is that it's cool, and it makes my jaw feel better. Actually, my jaw is feeling much better, and I begin to wonder if it's all psychosomatic and start thinking how to get out of paying for a clearly unnecessary mouthpiece. My raging credit-card debt is one of the banes of my existence, and I've got very little to show for it. It was mostly cash advances to pay for rent when Dana the Pillpopper spent all our money. I am so in the hole it's not funny, and now this dentist is going to extort me for another 650 bucks. This makes my heart pound, which in turn gets the jaw going, and I remind myself that there's no shortage of low-interest-rate credit cards. And if all else fails, I can always declare bankruptcy.

Finally, the imprints are done and I shuffle into the waiting room, rubbing my jaw. I find Lil in a corner, hunched over a *People* magazine. She looks drained. You could be having your leg amputated and Lil would find a way to make it all about her. "What's wrong?" I say, a little annoyed, considering this was supposed to be my turn to be the center of attention. She shakes her head. Doesn't want to talk about it. Fine by me. I toss a credit card from the Bank of Nebraska to the receptionist. And yet another card maxed. On the way out, I toss the Percocet prescription into the trash.

We step onto the elevator. Two business types step aside to make room for us. That's the extent of their acknowledgment. Then they turn back to their own thoughts, pretending no one is around them. And Lil decides to unburden herself. "That *fucker* Smith told me he was going out of town, but I have to look in *People* magazine and see that he's hosting a fucking benefit tonight! At the Plaza!"

Why Lil gets bent out of shape about these things is a mystery to me, but there's no use arguing with her when she gets like this. The suits are getting very uncomfortable. People don't like strong emotions. They like things to be simple and unfettered. They don't like to make waves. Lil, however, likes to make waves and I often get caught in the undertow. Which is exactly how it is that I come to be in the lobby of Smith's luxury apartment, five minutes later.

★

"I'm here to see Karl Malden."

This is the code name Smith has for himself. The doorman looks nervous. I feel bad for him. Forced by Lil into collusion. He leans in, discreet.

"*She's* here."

By she, I assume he means Smith's wife.

"I know. I'm not going *in*." And Lil stares at him until he waves us past.

We head up in a small, private elevator. It's carved entirely from walnut. A single recessed light pools onto the floor. It's all very dark, very dense, very demonic, very inside the specter. We arrive in a marble hallway and head out double French doors that lead to a terrace. I ask Lil *why* we're here but she's too pissed to answer. I go for levity—*where* are we? And she mutters something about a lower terrace, a private entrance, so that riffraff won't go traipsing through the main living area. I wonder aloud if this makes us riffraff, but Lil ignores me. I can see Central Park looming large—the view is spectacular—but Lil is too preoccupied by what's going on in the house to care about anything else. We head up a flight of stone steps and then she tells me to duck down. I watch as she hits the deck. I want to laugh but she's motioning for me to get down, as if we're in Nam and the place is crawling with Vietcong. She is making me very nervous. I quickly slide down next to her; the stone is cold, uninviting.

"We're gonna crawl across the terrace to get a better view," she hisses.

I freeze. Lil looks at me. I can tell she's irritated. I do some quick calculations in my head: This is crazy. Yet she took my wall drawing very well last night. Crazy versus friendship. My jaw throbs in tune to my thoughts. I unfreeze. We crawl across the terrace, military style.

Sliding past iron chaise lounges and exotic potted plants, we finally catch a glimpse of Mr. Smith. His wife is fixing his tie. There's a strange intimacy to it. It's probably something she's done a million times. She fixes his tie and he stands there patiently, like a good boy. I look over at Lil. She's seething. Seething over an old man who can't tie his own tie. He's got a paunch, age spots. Now I can see that he wears a toupee. The sun bounces off my watch and reminds me that I have to be at work in twenty minutes.

"Lil, I've gotta get out of here. Come on."

"No, I'm staying. I want to have a look-see once they leave."

This is Lil the thrill seeker, and I know better than to argue. Crawling back across the patio of one of the world's richest men, I think of Caroline and *La Femme Nikita*. I make a mental note to introduce Caroline and Lil, but then I think about the ramifications and I reconsider. I have always made it a rule to keep all my worlds from colliding. And despite the fact that I know Caroline could use a little thrill seeking in her life, I'm not willing to give her Lil.

SEVEN

I get to the bar five minutes late for my shift and Tommy, the blustery alcoholic, is screaming at me before I'm halfway through the door. I put my hands up, a "what can you do" gesture, and say, "I'm sorry. I was in tort class; Al Gore was the guest speaker; I just couldn't get out."

Everyone at work thinks I'm in law school because when I interviewed for the job, Tommy, making polite conversation, asked me what I did with myself. Instead of saying something vague, something noncommittal, I announced that I was in law school. He was impressed. He blabbed it to everyone else, as if I were his kid and he were the proud father. It was a mistake, but I just didn't want to tell him the truth. Sometimes I replay the moment in my mind: Tommy asks me what I do with myself, and I speak honestly and openly. I tell him that I am a twenty-five-year-old conservatory dropout who has just finished cohabitating with a pill-popping egomaniac. I would include the fact that I have spent years of my life studying an art form that I have recently quit and that in the interim, I have come to the realization that in addition to having no marketable skills, I have no prospects.

In short, Tom, I am a failure.

My lie nags at me because I've grown friendly with some of the girls I work with. But I know I'll never be able to stay friends with them because our friendship, or at least the details of my life, are somewhat predicated on a lie. Lil finds my lies to be endearing. But Lil has been listening to them since we were kids. She was there at the beginning when I told all the cute boys in school that my brother could stick a motorcycle spoke through his arm and hang a bucket of water from it while standing on broken glass. They were impressed, and it was all well and good, until one day when a few of the guys decided to stop by to watch my brother do his thing. I actually tried to convince my brother, who was ten at the time, to do it, but he wouldn't. I was desperate, and they knew I had lied. When they left, the first person I called was Lil. I didn't even know her that well, but I called her and I told her what I had done. And she laughed. She just laughed. After that no one talked to me for a while, but Lil and I became best friends. In the interim I've told a thousand lies. I've told people that I was a pig farmer; I've told people that I was in the Olympics; I've told people that I was a jockey. I don't think they believed me.

I think I'd stop lying if I could find something good to be honest about.

Tommy finishes his tirade. Something about making an ex-ample out of me. I head into the back, numb, and marry half-filled bottles of ketchup until my shift begins.

★

The place fills up pretty quickly, and I fall into the rhythm eas-ily enough. I don't usually have this shift, so I don't know the girls too well. Most of them are from Queens. They're a tough bunch. They say "Yo" a lot. But I recognize the customers. College guys, stockbrokers, a few bridge-and-tunnel types from the Island. And the jukebox is good tonight. I realize I haven't listened to any music since my last shift. It seems these days, it's the only time I can bear to hear a song. Sly and the Family Stone are blaring and suddenly I'm filled with nostalgia, but for what I can't remember. I only know that while the song lasts I'm filled with an overall sense of happiness. I get five ta-bles at once. I'm totally running on autopilot at this point.

Four bars into the next song and I think about my first gui-tar. Some relic my father forgot to take after the divorce. I think of my father playing the guitar, humming a tune as he played along. My father had perfect pitch, he could learn a tune just by listening to it, and my aunt was a prodigy. She was performing at Lincoln Center by the time she was ten. But according to family lore, she became an alcoholic lounge singer who packed a pistol and changed her name from Marie to Lonnie—a black man's name, is what my mother always says. Although I've never met any black men named Lonnie. I haven't spoken to my father or my aunt in a million years. Neither one ever called me after the divorce; they never sought me out; there were no birthday cards with crisp dollar bills inside. Nothing. They just moved on. We all have our crosses to bear; that's one of mine. Although the fact that my father played music and my aunt was a prodigy makes me think that maybe I'm rejecting Humphrey because it's my only way of rejecting them. All this while waiting for John the bartender to pour me five pints of Bass Ale for the table full of budding alcoholics in the corner. I deliver said beers.

"Hey, are you an actress?"

The one in the striped button-down oxford shirt asks. I smile but don't answer. I don't have the energy to lie tonight. I pass my tables, survey the landscape. One of the neon lamps in the Miller beer sign is buzzing. Three old guys at the bar are arguing about the longshoreman's union. Two waitresses are standing next to the computer, trying to find a button. Peaches the night porter has just walked in with a huge pail full of ice because the freezer's on the fritz. My work for the moment is done, and I suddenly think of Lil in her Elvis suit. I think of the two of us stealing that plasma screen, I think of Stockbroker Guy asleep in the chair, I think of the fart that clinched the plasma screen, and I burst out laughing, aware of the fact that to everyone else, I look like a lunatic. And then, just like that, I stop. I go from sixty to zero in two seconds flat. I freeze.

M is sitting in the corner of my little bar. He is alone, with nothing but a pint of Guinness in front of him.

M, here, right now.

I panic, then I calm down, then I panic again. Christine from Queens has just taken his order. I catch her at the bar.

"Did he say anything?"

"Who?"

"The guy you just took an order from."

"Nah, he just ordered a pint. He's got a weird accent."

I look at her. Dumbfounded. "Don't you know who he is?"

She doesn't. "Do you want the table?"

I think for a moment. I can't serve M! It would confuse *everything*. And yet I'm so in love with him. Seeing him here just confirms it. But do I want to meet him like this? Inevitably he'll ask me a question and I'll lie and then I'll never be able to be totally comfortable with him because my lies will come back to haunt me at every turn. I will die filled with regret that my life with him was built on falsehoods and deceit.

"No."

Instead I call Lil. I'm inches away from him as I call. He's reading *About Schmidt,* only one of my most favorite books. It's absolute *kismet* and I can't do anything! The machine picks up. Lil's not home, she's still at Smith's. I hang up and sigh a quiet little sigh. The most amazing thing has happened and I have no one to share it with. I go back to work, because what else can I do? He stays about an hour and the entire time I'm careful. I make no eye contact with him, although I walk past him about twenty times. I don't want him having any sense of me as a waitress. I don't make jokes, I don't sing along to "I Will Survive" when everyone else does. I don't talk to the other waitresses. I just work.

And then he leaves, and I go into the bathroom and throw up.

After my shift, I walk home slowly, wondering where he is. He must be around here somewhere, and maybe if I walk slowly enough I'll happen upon him. I'm afraid I'll never see him again. I start brooding. Maybe I should've talked to him? He was reading *About Schmidt*! What are the odds of *that*? I *should* have talked to him. I could have told him that I love the book! But then I would've been just another chatty waitress, and I don't want him to think of me as that. I want him to think of me as better than that. Even though the fact is, I'm not.

My stomach is in knots. I finally get home, brimming with anticipation that Lil will be there, but there's no sign of her. I'm in the big loft all by myself. I put *Last Emperor* into the VCR. I take off my smelly bar clothes and put on a pair of pajama bottoms and a halter top. I pile my hair up and open a pack of smokes. I will stay up all night if I have to. I cannot go to bed without telling Lil. I will kill time; it's something I'm good at. I pull out my copy of *About Schmidt* from a cardboard box in the closet. I prop it up on the kitchen counter. Then I grab a pen. I want to write about this but nothing comes out. It's all still happening. I can't process it. Nothing comes out.

I hit Play and *Last Emperor* comes to life on the screen. I've seen it so many times now, but I don't have the energy to get the other movie out of the box. So I just put my aching feet into the kitchen sink and run some cold water over them. The water doubles as a receptacle for my ashes. John Lone, swathed in red. Lil's right, he is a piece of ass, but she's not here. What can I do to make her come home? I see Humphrey facing the boxes of paper in the corner.

Humphrey always has the answers. Smug bastard that he is. I will get rid of the origami paper and in doing so, Lil will return. I never used to be this superstitious, but what the hell. Why not give it a try? I reach for the first box, thinking how this is just like throwing away two hundred dollars, when the top falls off, and I see the paper. Alizarin crimson. A lush, vibrant red, just like the one in the movie. It's exactly the same.

And suddenly, I have a change of heart.

I place the top piece on the southern wall near the windows. I tack it up, and then I stare at it, this red rectangle. It brings me such peace that I'm left craving more. So I open the other boxes. The crisp sheets of colored paper sigh, as if they needed air to come to life. I take a single piece from each box and tack them in a line on the wall. I do this without thought, or rather without intent. I just like the way the colors look more than anything. When I finish, I step back to admire the line. But the colors seem out of joint, jumbled. Something isn't right. I spend an hour moving them, until they seem to make more sense.

EIGHT

Yellow, gray, blue, red, white, purple, green, orange, black, pink, brown, and light blue. A simple line of twelve pieces of colored paper on the wall. And a strange sense of satisfaction comes over me, as if the complexity of my emotions have somehow been distilled into pure, luminous tones that seem to vibrate against the stark white of the wall. It's all very Ellsworth Kelly. I think even Bonnie Cashin would approve.

I collapse on the window seat. If a watched pot never boils, I am the water inside. Lil is not coming home tonight. My M sighting will have to wait. The entire thing falls into strange and sudden perspective, and I realize that it all meant nothing.

M was just there.

Nothing more.

I think about writing some words on the wall, but I can't summon the energy to get up. The whole city is sleeping except for me. I look out at all the lights and feel horribly alone. All of us in our apartments and nothing connecting us except the collective beating of our hearts and the shared consumption of the dark city air. I roll back to John Lone, but my mind thinks only of M. I imagine that I am lying next to him, his warm breath falling on my neck. I would give anything for his warm breath on the back of my neck. I shut my eyes and pray for sleep to come over me fast while on-screen the eunuchs are trying to kill the emperor.

★

The phone rings, and I wake up with a start. It's Mr. Smith.

"Please come to my office at once."

And before I can clear my throat to ask why, he tells me.

"Lil has been kidnapped."

NINE

Which makes no sense. It's utterly inconceivable.

Yet somehow it has happened.

The traffic going uptown is horrendous, so I endlessly review everything Smith told me in our brief phone conversation. She was kidnapped. They thought she was his daughter because apparently, she was sleeping in his daughter's bed. My zooming mind sticks on this for a while—*What* was she *doing*? The image is oddly perverted, like some sort of incestuous Goldilocks—then races back into the loop. They called his office to announce the kidnapping, but the real daughter was sitting in the office with him. He thought nothing of it; then an hour later a Polaroid of Lil arrived. They still think she's his daughter. He, of course, wants this kept quiet. After his last affair, his wife had the paperwork changed. One billion dollars is at stake, and if she finds out, it all goes to her. He'll lose his shirt, literally. He kept using words like *discretion* and *privacy*.

The call was like a bad, teeth-grinding anxiety dream. Only it was real.

I get to his building, throw money at the cab driver, and head inside. I get in the elevator and take it all the way to the top floor. Canned music is being pumped in through some small speaker hidden somewhere. It's an obscure guitar etude by a Spanish composer no one normal knows. I know it, because I performed it twice. I think about the odds of me hearing it and decide that they're just low enough to make this ride fraught with irony. Or maybe not irony but *something* strange.

When I arrive, the woman at the desk looks at me funny. I realize I'm still in my pajamas. It hits me for real then: My best friend has been kidnapped! I'm trying to stay calm but I'm having visions of torture and rape, and I have to shove them out of my head. I remind myself that Lil takes shit from no one. Lil is not a victim. Lil will be all right. I give my name and I'm ushered into Mr. Smith's office immediately. I'm sure everyone wonders what my connection to him is, but they don't dare acknowledge the curiosity. Lil says that every employee is forced to sign a confidentiality waiver thus keeping Mr. Smith's secrets safe.

He doesn't bother to get up from his desk when I enter. I notice that he's actually looking over a contract. I cough so he sees me, and he tosses it down.

"That Lil, she's a handful."

I don't quite know how to respond to this. And why is he

alone? Where are the authorities? Who is taking action here? "Have you heard from the kidnappers again? Have you called the police, the FBI?" I hear myself blurt.

He looks at me for a long moment. As if he's putting me in some sort of mind meld. "There'll be none of that. My people are handling the security issues. Obviously we don't want this getting out to the press. Or to anyone in my family."

I want to scream at him. But I can't. The words are all lined up but they can't get out.

"I have spoken to the kidnappers." He gives me a tight smile.

Relief comes over me.

"And you're going to function as the go-between."

"What?!"

"I have given them your phone number and they will call you with further instructions."

"But . . . I'm not good with confrontation," I say meekly. Is he crazy? He's *not* calling the police?

"Well, I suspect you will be when all of this is finished."

"But Mr. Smith—"

He looks at me funny; I realize he doesn't know we call him Smith.

"*I* can't do this. We have to call in the cops, the professionals; she's been *kidnapped*!"

"We're going to get her back. They're going to want money, I'm going to give it to you, and you're going to deliver it." He picks up a file, pages through it.

Doesn't this guy ever watch TV? Has he not seen even one episode of *La Femme Nikita*? "It *never* works like that.

There's *always* a catch. Or she's already dead and they're going to run off with the cash and we'll never find her!" I lose my breath at this thought. He ignores me and hands me a piece of paper casually.

"I'm going to need you to sign this."

A confidentiality agreement. "You're joking."

He narrows his gaze. "I have a corporation to run. Lives depend on it. I have thousands of salaried employees; I have commitments; I have a responsibility to my workers."

He's got a responsibility to keep one billion dollars from his wife. What a piece of shit. A mental note forms. When this is over, Lil is to dump him immediately. I grab the agreement. It says something about lawsuits and indemnity and litigation and blah blah blah. . . . I just sign it. Parker Grey.

I hand it back to him. And I smile to myself because Parker Grey isn't my real name. I changed my name because it was boring and regular. It had no ring to it. But I never changed it legally. Smith doesn't know this. He's got nothing on me.

"They will be calling this evening."

"This evening I have to work."

"I'm sure you'll find a way out of it."

And I truly hate him. I hate him because he has more money than God, and I barely earn enough to buy eggs. I hate him because Lil has been kidnapped, and I don't think he gives a shit. On my way out, he calls to me.

"I *am* upset about this. I really am. But I didn't get this far by allowing life's little curveballs to rattle me."

★

Back at home, I put on my best sore throat voice and I call in sick. But Tommy isn't buying it.

"Get your fucking ass in here, or I'm shit-canning you!"

He hangs up.

The phone rings immediately. Maybe it's Tommy with a change of heart. I answer. But it's not.

"Who is this?"

"Don't ask questions." They sound nervous.

"Okay."

"We want money."

My heart is beating so loud I'm sure they can hear it. "How much?"

There's a pause. I hear low voices muttering. They don't sound very together.

"Just get the money, or we'll kill her."

And that sounds real. It sounds really real, and my mouth goes dry. My knees begin to shake involuntarily. "I will. How much and where and . . . when?"

The guy has his hand over the receiver. I can hear fighting. It's like there's dissension or something, not good. They're nervous, they're panicked, they could do something stupid. And I'm freaking out. I can't do this. I. Can't. Do. This. I pull myself together. "Listen, hello? Hello?"

"What."

"I can get you the money. We'll just agree to a drop-off place and you guys can, you know, take the money, and I'll take Lil."

"Who the fuck is Lil?"

They think she's Smith's daughter, right. "Just tell me how much—"

"We haven't decided yet."

Christ. I don't know where to go from here. Typically, they have a figure in mind. At least, they do on TV. It takes all my nerve to issue forth my next sentence. "I'll need to see her first." I cringe as I say it. I don't want to make them angry. *Please don't be angry*—

"Fuck you! *No!* We get the money first, then if everything's okay, we'll let her go."

"But I'll need proof that she's alive and okay. Let me talk to her! Please—"

"Shut up! Get one thing straight. You call the cops and I cut her in half with a fucking serrated knife."

And then I hear Lil in the background. *"Where the fuck is Smith?!?"*

"We'll call you later with the figure."

And they hang up. The line goes dead. Just like that, she's gone. Now what? *Later?* I have to go to work but I can't leave the phone. I can't leave the phone, but I have to go to work. I can't lose this job because it's spring, and there are no others. I can't lose the job. I have to lose the job. They're going to cut Lil in half with a serrated knife.

And I start to cry.

I let it all out, and I know it's not just for Lil. It's residual buildup that's been waiting for a chance to break. With each tear I feel myself slipping away. Defragmenting into a million tiny, wet drops all over the floor. I'm shattering into pieces. I see my spleen crawling away. I am a remnant of a person I barely knew. All that's left are vague impressions and hazy recollections that might as well belong to someone else. I feel no connection to the present or the past. I am only here, in the kitchen, in a million pieces, clinging for my life to a cold Formica countertop.

Salt and snot and years of pent-up frustration.

And it occurs to me that none of this seems very real. It's almost as if this isn't actually happening to me. It's almost as if it's part of a show. A big show. Maybe it's called *Life*. No, it can't be *Life*. That would be a miniseries. This is definitely a weekly thing. One hour at a pop. I'm thinking seven seasons and then I can live on forever in syndication.

I'm getting calmer.

Okay, I think, breathing a deep breath. This is *The Parker Grey Show*. And while I cannot handle it, Parker Grey can. Parker Grey can do anything. I wipe my snot away with a dirty dishrag. Then I stare out my giant, clean windows. I wonder who's out there and if anyone's watching, because at this stage, I really don't want to be canceled. I must not worry about ratings. I must focus only on my character. I must focus on the story at hand. One more deep, cleansing breath. I am in character now.

And for the first time since I can remember, I am fine.

I am going to work. I will activate the call-forwarding feature that Lil wisely took on our phone plan. I'll be in the front section of the bar tonight, and the waitress in the front is responsible for taking all incoming calls on the pay phone. A simple Out of Order sign on the phone will keep customers from using it.

I can be there.

I can answer the phone.

I can work, thus not losing my job, which I am supposed to be at in twenty minutes. I look like hell, but there's no time to shower. I scrub my face with some concoction that Lil got at Mario Badescu. It sloughs off a layer and I rub on a ton of lotion. At least now my skin is glowing. I throw my hair up. Lip balm, mascara, a shot of Right Guard under the pits, and I'm out the door. But I've forgotten something. I run back in and grab the silver pen with the thick velvety tip and write along the top of the beam: "STAY TUNED FOR MORE AFTER THE BREAK."

TEN

Lenny the bartender doesn't usually have this shift. It is my bad luck that he's subbing for Doc, who is very easygoing and relaxed. Lenny, however, is a lunatic micromanager, and putting an Out of Order sign on the bar's pay phone is simply too much for him to bear. He asks lots of questions because, although he's a powerless man, he is in a position of power, and breaking balls is something he is an expert at. Right now, he is reaching a dangerous level of irritation over what he has taken to calling "the phone situation."

I have to think fast.

Lenny is a high school dropout from Syosset. He believes in conspiracies and aliens and he thinks the Feds are after the two guys who own the bar. This belief stems from the fact that both owners may be involved with the mob. I don't know all the details, but I do know that one of the owners, Tommy Sr., has spent time "upstate." I once made the mistake of asking him if he enjoyed the fishing.

Lenny is staring at me with his bulging conspiracy-theory eyes. And in an instant I know what do to. Of course. It's so simple. I look around for effect, as if I'm afraid someone might overhear. Then I lean in. Discreet, almost furtive. "About ten minutes ago some creepy *cocksucker* came in here—"

Lenny responds to these kinds of descriptions.

"—and he's acting all casual. He tells me he's a stockbroker. He's making chitchat . . . . *But the thing is,* I saw him earlier, when I was walking to work. Bastard was sitting *inside a van* drinking a cup of coffee with three other guys. And when he opened the door to the van, there was all sorts of recording equipment—"

"Feds?!"

Lenny's Geiger counter is going berserk. I remain calm.

"I don't want to say, Len, but all I know is, five minutes later, he's in here telling me he's a 'stockbroker.' "

"What the *fuck*?"

I look around once more. "I saw him mess with the phone."

"Get the fuck out!"

"I don't want to get involved, I don't want to know anything, but when I see something fucked up like that . . ." Lenny is buying this. My Emmy nomination is imminent. "It's just not American."

Lenny is moved.

"This isn't Russia." Lenny also hates communists.

"Fuckin' A, Parker! It's a good thing I didn't see him, I'll tell you that, 'cause I woulda taken a fucking bat to his head—"

"So, *that's* why I put the Out of Order sign on the phone. Keep *everyone* off it so they have nothing to listen to."

"I'm with you on that. *Fuck them.* Bunch of cocksucker bastards."

Lenny has a low IQ and he has trouble with logic. If the Feds were bugging the phone, patron calls really wouldn't affect a case against the two bozos who own the bar. He hasn't made that connection. And for this I am grateful.

"It's best to keep this kind of stuff to ourselves, Parker."

What does he mean by this? "Who would I tell?"

"Alls I'm saying is that it might be best if we kept this between the two of us. We don't want Tommy or Tommy Sr. getting worried that too many people know about the inner workings of their business. . . ."

Lenny, I realize with some admiration, is trying to cut me out so he can tell Tommy Sr. and reap the glory for having spotted the nonexistent Fed bugging the phone. "That's fine with me, Lenny."

"So, we're agreed, the phone business is on the q.t."

"What phone business?"

It takes him a second to get it. Then he laughs.

"That's good, Parker. 'What phone business?' That's funny stuff."

★

Two hours and there's still no call. The bar is packed. I wade back and forth through the bodies, bringing beer to the huddled masses. Snippets of meaningless conversations float in the air: "... *I really think Sheryl Crow has a lot to answer for.*" I'm listening. "... *Fucking girl had the best rack.*" I'm not listening. "... *So we get there and I tell him I don't eat meat and he gets all snippy with me....*"

I check the phone. Lift it up to make sure it has a dial tone and then slam it back down because I fear that they may be trying to get through at this very second. Lenny sees me. He thinks I'm goofing around. He's winking at me and doing a lot with hand signals as if he's my new best friend. I bring beer, I fetch beer. I try to tune out the endless drone of the extras. After all, I repeat to myself when I feel my nerves, this is my show not theirs. "... *I mean she got her start in Las Vegas and then she leaves and she gets a big new producer and her old manager fucking blows his brains out and she doesn't care....*"

"... *So I like him but I don't know. Do you think he's going to call? Because he said he was going to call....*"

Finally, the phone rings. I bolt. There's a drunken asshole nearby, and I know he's going to go for it. Drunks in bars just love to answer pay phones, as if it's the wackiest random thing they can do. I spill beer all over myself in my mad lunge, and what doesn't land on me goes on the floor. And I slip in it. One of those jerk-your-head-back kind of slips where you think you're going down for sure, but somehow you manage to propel your body forward.

I grab the phone.

"*Yes!*"

"You're home? It's so loud. Are you having a party?"

It's my mother.

"Mom, I'm actually at work—"

"That's funny, because I called your home number—"

"I know, I'm forwarding the calls—"

"Why would you do that?"

Jesus, I can't take this. "Mom, it's too hard to explain, I was just expecting a call and I didn't want to miss it."

"Really?"

It's the tone that gets me. That Mom tone. She says "really," but she's actually saying something else.

"A new boy?"

Christ. "No, Mom, *not* a new boy. I just promised Lil I'd take a message for her."

My mom gets quiet. She knows I'm lying, but she can't even begin to imagine the real story. This is irritating to her.

"Mom, I've got to go. I can't talk now." Some idiot puts on Pearl Jam, and I have to cover my ears to hear her response.

"I'm worried about you."

These are my mother's four favorite words.

"Mom, please." My standard response.

"No, I am. You're not playing your music, you've a wonderful talent, and I see you in the city, all alone, having a crisis and I'm worried."

I don't know what she wants me to say. "Please don't worry. I'm fine. I swear."

"I want you to call Dan Armbrewster."

Dan Armbrewster is a shrink friend of the family. "I'm not calling Dan, Mom. You go out to dinner with Dan."

"He's assured me that he'll be discreet."

"The fact that he's assuring you at all is problematic to me."

"Please call him."

"Mom, I have to go."

"Okay, but I love you. And I'm worried about you. And don't forget to call your stepfather next week; it's his birthday. Make a fuss, he likes that—"

I am ready to kill myself. "Mom, I've got to go. Love you." I hang up.

Then I stare at the clock, hoping to Christ they didn't just try.

★

Eleven o'clock and still no call. And things couldn't be worse. Some crazy old bastard named Frank has shat himself at the bar. Shat as in past tense of shit. The bouncers are all very understanding; apparently he's been having colon issues. There's a long huddle and suddenly it's agreed that since the shit happened in my section, I should clean it up. I remind them that people often vomit here, yet none of the waitresses are required to clean *that* up. They don't know what to do, and the stench is horrible. I suggest they reconvene. After another group huddle, it's agreed that Peaches, the thug night porter, who's downstairs in the beer cellar probably smoking crack, should do it.

The catch is that I have to tell him.

It's nearly eleven-thirty. The phone has not rung. I am tired. I am worried. And now I have to tell an angry, crack-smoking Neanderthal who has issues with both authority and women that he has to clean up a pile of shit. I calculate that this will take two minutes. I tell Laurel that I'm expecting a really important call and that she has to answer the phone. Laurel is stoned; she's wearing the fry cook's clear Plexiglas goggles. "Isn't this hilarious! I've been wearing them for an hour. I told the customers it's a new OSHA standard thing."

Laurel promises to answer the phone for me. She may be stoned, but she can be counted on. I head through the kitchen, into the giant freezer, and down the rickety steps to the cellar. I reach the bottom rung and hear a low growl that quickly turns into a snarl. It's Peaches's pit bull, Boomer. I've always considered myself to be a dog person. I've grown up with dogs, loved dogs, admired dogs. But this dog hates me in a way that I've never been hated before. There's no doubt he's going to attack. I bolt back up the steps, but Boomer is hot on my tail.

I jump onto one of the counters and then climb onto the shelf where they keep the giant bowls and the beer batter mix. The dog is losing his mind, trying to get on the counter. I'm screaming my head off. *"Somebody!!"* But I'm in the goddamn freezer and no one can hear me. *"Help me!!!!"* I look down and hiss, "Fuck you, Boomer." This only pisses him off more. All of his hair is standing on edge. I'm throwing pots at him and bowls, bags of flour and beer-batter mix. Anything I can get my hands on. And then the door opens. It's Peaches. He sees the dog covered in batter and flour.

"What the fuck are you doing to *my dog?!*"

To the normal person, the situation would be clear.

Peaches, however, is turning purple with rage. Boomer instantly whines like a baby and runs into his master's arms. I don't move. "Please get him out of here," I say, trying for a tone of dignity and calm. Peaches shakes his head slowly and glares at me. He looks frightening. There is absolutely no way I'm going to tell him about the shit. He curses to himself in Spanish and heads out with the dog.

I jump down and hear the phone ringing. On my show, my clumsiness is considered endearing and quirky. But here I know the fry cook will scream at me for making a mess. All this and I didn't even tell Peaches to clean up the fecal matter. The phone! I have to get to the phone!

I race past the grill. Laurel is pulling burgers off the slide. *"Hey, I think the phone is ringing. . . ."* My heart is about to explode, I round the corner and who do I see?

M.

The sight of him jars me to a stop. Just long enough to register the moment. And in that fraction of a second, our eyes meet. And the look on my face is pure, unadulterated shock working on ten different levels, I'm sure. But I can still hear the phone ringing, and I have to keep moving, and so I do. I'm not even sure I really stopped. But those eyes, staring at me. It was something.

I reach the phone. Grab it. Totally out of breath.

"Yeah . . ."

I catch a glimpse of the vision that is me in the mirror over the bar. I am covered in batter and flour. My hair is matted to the side of my head. My sweaty face is beet red.

"We want you to get two million dollars by tomorrow."

"Two million. Okay." I nod. Pocket change for Mr. Smith.

There's a long pause. I'm terrified they're going to start expecting me to have all the answers about things like pickups and drop-offs. Then I remind myself that I am the hero, not the villain. The hero never has to say where the money is supposed to be dropped.

"Be at the pay phone outside Elephant and Castle on Greenwich tomorrow morning at ten-fifteen. We'll contact you with instructions from there."

The old wait-by-the-pay-phone-for-a-call routine. I've seen it before.

"Is she okay?"

"For now."

The line goes dead.

All I have to do is get the money from Mr. Smith. I fumble in my pocket for the number he gave me and dial. "They called!"

"Yes."

He's so calm. I guess that's why he's a mogul.

"They want two million dollars tomorrow. I'm supposed to go—"

He cuts me off. "I don't want to know the details."

Smith always looks out for number one.

"You will call me once you know where the drop-off is to occur, I will have the money delivered to you then, and you will deliver it."

My mind is racing. Smith is acting like this is some everyday deal that happens all the time. But I'm clueless. "I have a question."

"Yes?"

"How do I get her back? Aren't I supposed to demand to get her at the same time as I give the money?"

"Once they have the money, there will be no reason to keep Lil. They will return her and this mess will be over."

He seems so confident that I decide to believe him, although I have a nagging sensation in the back of my mind. She can identify them; she knows who they are. What's to stop her from going after them? But I can't think about that. I have to have faith that Lil is okay because the best friend is always okay, at least they're usually okay. I hang up.

I'm worn out. I'm dirty and I'm tired.

And M is in the next room.

From the doorway, I can see that Esme is leaning against his table, and her foot is doing that cutsie little wiggle thing that it does when she's flirting, and I find myself getting very angry. I stand at the bar, unable to move. She saunters over, hops up, and calls her order to Lenny.

"Did you see that guy in there, Parker?"

I act stupid. "What guy?"

"That guy over on six. He's an actor. I've seen him on *Doctors*."

He's not on *Doctors*, he's on *MEDS*. But I say nothing.

"He's sooo hot. He's in town because he's shooting a movie. It's called *True North*."

Esme knows more about M than I do. This stings. I feel myself losing faith. I love M. M doesn't love me.

"He's got such a sexy accent. I think he's Russian."

"He's Croatian."

"So you know who I'm talking about then?"

I nod. "Yeah, I know who you're talking about."

"I'm going to go flirt with him. Ten bucks says that he's going to ask me out before the night's over."

I'm ready to cry. "You're on."

★

I spend the rest of the shift delivering beer. Drunken customers keep saying things to me like, "Cheer up," or "It can't be so bad." But it is. It's worse. Maybe my mother's right, I should see a shrink. On the upside, the pity tip thing has taken hold, and I rake in a small fortune—relatively speaking. But for what? We live and then we die and in between not much makes sense. My best friend is being held for ransom and I am killing time, waiting for my life to begin, and I'm starting to think it will never happen. I'm slipping into an existential funk. I tell myself it's stress over the drop-off, but in reality, it's M. Pathetic me. I would like my character to be stronger, bur alas, she is vulnerable and sensitive.

When the shift ends, I count out my money.

Esme sidles up to me and hands me ten bucks. "Bastard didn't bite. Nothing. I swear, these actors. They're so vague and tortured. Who needs it?"

I take the ten in my hand. Cool and crisp. And a wave of hope washes over me. Suddenly everything is okay again, or at least as okay as can be, considering.

★

I go home and stand in the shower until my skin turns pink. Then I hear the phone ringing, but I don't have the energy to get out of the water until a most unpleasant thought enters my head.

What if it's about Lil?

I quickly lean my head out of the curtain just as the machine picks up.

"Hey . . . Where are you? I've been thinking about you. I just read this book about children of divorce. . . . I'm dying to talk to you about it."

It's only Trudy, leaving another one of her rambling messages. I should call her back, but I just can't talk to anyone right now. I stick my head back under the water, but I can still hear her voice bouncing off the walls of the apartment.

"Come see me up at the Marriott; I'm working every night this week. Hope you're okay; it's not like you to not call back. . . ."

ELEVEN

It is early in the morning, and I'm sticking origami paper on the wall. Amazingly relaxed, still high off the fact that M wasn't interested in Esme, I pull out the different colored sheets and glue them on. The tacks were a distraction. They were creating too much space around themselves and in doing so they interrupted the flow of the colors. The flow of the harmony. The white walls are slowly disappearing, and along with them my fear and anxiety about today's phone call. I am surrounding myself with color and beauty. I am hoping secretly that at some point this jumbled mass of color will come to life and pull me inside. I'm tempted to put on some music but Humphrey might take that as a sign of weakness. Instead, I paste the papers as if I am some modern-day Matisse, expressing my repressed, or rather depressed, creativity onto some bizarre palette.

At nine-thirty, I calmly change my clothes and head to Elephant and Castle on Greenwich. I'm there by ten and the phone is already ringing.

"Yes?"

"Where the fuck have you been?!"

"You said ten-*fifteen*."

"We said ten!"

This is an argument that I will not win, so I don't bother.

"This was a test to see if you could follow directions."

"Ah."

"Do you have the money?"

"Not on me! But I can get it!"

"Be on the corner of Avenue A and First at twelve sharp. You will be contacted. And look at the package taped to the bottom of this phone booth."

They hang up. My hands are trembling as I reach under the phone booth. I can feel a small, flat package taped there. I pull it loose and tear it open. Inside there's a single Polaroid of Lil. She looks a little tired, but I know she's all right because she has her head tilted so that her good side is showing. I feel a flood of relief, and then I'm suddenly annoyed. If she's vain enough to be concerned about taking a good photo, she's okay, and maybe I have been worrying for nothing. Smith was right; they want the money, nothing more. And, I realize, I'm also irritated by the fact that now I have to schlep all the way over to the East Village. Clearly, the kidnappers want to turn my show into a bad sitcom. I take a deep, calming breath and admit to myself that not every episode can be inspired.

And then I walk to the East Village.

I pass at least ten people along the way who are carrying guitars. I try to remember exactly why I walked away from playing, but I can't. There was a time when I loved it. I loved to play music. I loved everything about it. Everything flowed. Everything. All day long, I ate, drank, and breathed music. Even when I slept, there was a constant cacophony. I got so used to hearing the voicings inside my head, I didn't think anything of it.

Until one day they all stopped.

Things just went wrong. I'd like to blame it on entropy, but mostly I blame myself, because at some point I stopped trusting my instincts. It became about everyone else and not about the music. I spent years of my life learning to play lull-abies to the cultural elite, and I never wanted that. I wanted to study music so that I could have roots. I wanted to learn everything so that I could forget it all. But I got caught up in something else. I listened to too many people and I stopped following my own instincts. I cut up Ludlow Street.

I once had a gig at the Ludlow Street Café, back when I had some vision. It was a little dive. I wrote some music, got a couple of percussionists and singers to do a few rehearsals, and then I hung up signs. The Pillpopper was livid. How could I possibly embarrass him by performing in such a shit hole? But I was undeterred. For whatever reason, the place was packed. I was so in the zone I barely remember anything. I do remember feeling as if I were nothing more than a con-duit. Music just spilling through me and out of Humphrey. And it was all mine. It was my music and for that night, my band. Three percussionists, a bass player named Stomu, two singers, even Lil was in on it, manning an overhead projector, flashing all these crazy photos that we'd cut out of a magazine and pasted together. And it took on a life of its own. It was great. It was fun and hyper and kinesthetic. And the audience totally responded because it was like nothing else. Because it was pure. Pure me.

What I didn't know was that a Japanese record executive had shown up. He came to hear another band, but there was a scheduling mix-up, and he ended up hearing me instead. And he liked what he heard. But I didn't know this. I didn't know any of it, because Dana spoke to him. And Dana didn't want me doing better than him. So when the Japanese record executive gave him his card to give to me, Dana threw it out. I never called because I never knew.

It was a year before I found out. I ran into a guy who had been at the show. I didn't even know him. But he remembered me. He had heard the Japanese man talking to Dana the Pillpopper. He had heard the whole conversation, and he remembered. He remembered because he said he was sure that he was going to be seeing my CD in the stores soon. Imagine my reaction, hearing all of this from a perfect stranger on the corner of Christopher Street and Seventh.

I went home and threw up.

I confronted the Pillpopper, and he denied it. So I packed all my stuff into a suitcase, grabbed Humphrey, and left. Maybe nothing would have come of it. But I know that night at Ludlow Street was something special. I went someplace I hadn't been before. And afterward, I couldn't seem to go anywhere. Dana suddenly switched into high gear, popping Percocet like Pez. And it was all I could do to stay sane.

I reach the corner of First and A and am overwhelmed by the stench of piss just as a car drives by and a newspaper is thrown at me. I duck. *Who the hell would throw a newspaper at me?* But then I realize that it's them. My kidnapper friends. I grab the paper and open it. Scrawled on the page are the words: "Be at the diner on Christopher Street at 3:30 for further instructions."

I call Smith from a pay phone. He tells me to call again at 3:30, at which point he'll send a car, and the driver will give me the money. He says that this is for my own protection; he doesn't want me wandering around with two million dollars cash. I don't argue with him.

I walk back west and up Seventh Avenue to Christopher. I'm really worn out. Exhausted. I realize I haven't had a smoke in about two hours, and I'm going into withdrawal. I light up as I pass the Time Café. What am I going to do between now and 3:30?

"Parker?" I look up and see Caroline hanging over the railing of the upstairs outdoor terrace. "Come have lunch with me! You have to meet my friend Vaughn; he's a hoot." She smiles that big Cheshire grin of hers. Then she flashes an Amex card. "Expense account, baby!"

I laugh, because she knows that I am completely intrigued by this expense account of hers. I waver for a brief moment, wondering about protocol. Is it poor form to have lunch in order to kill time while I wait to collect two million dollars and make a drop-off to save my best friend? I think of Lil and her warped socialist tendencies. By using the expense account, she would argue, we are in our own little way redistributing some of the wealth. And, I remind myself, she did make sure her best side was showing in the Polaroid, so her peril is not so great. Plus, I reason, and this is the clincher, I am the star of this show, and the hero always stops for lunch. I head up the steps, and Caroline waves me over to her table. She is smoking up a storm.

"This is great! I can't *believe* I saw you. Sit . . ."

I pull up a seat. Caroline's wearing a retro-looking dress with lots of yellow in it, and white go-go boots that must have belonged to her mother. On anyone else, this would look ridiculous. On her it looks, for lack of a better word, groovy.

"I think I'm going to become an alcoholic. I'm viewing it as a career choice," she says, drinking what looks like a martini.

I opt for a Diet Coke with extra lemon.

"So, what are you up to?"

"Just running errands." I leave it at that, even though I know Caroline would like nothing more than to be an accessory to a crime. I sip my Diet Coke, and then Vaughn arrives. He's wearing red velvet pants, and as Caroline makes the introductions he looks down and spots something on my skirt. "Is that an attached pocket purse?"

I like him already for noticing. I am indeed wearing a blue miniskirt with an attached pocket purse that I sewed on myself. I smile. "It's one of my many tributes to Bonnie Cashin."

"Bonnie Cashin?"

I nod.

"Bonnie Cashin, *the* famed costume and clothing designer? Inventor of the Coach bag?"

"That's the one."

He looks at Caroline. "Where have you been hiding her?"

Caroline is pleased. She feigns a shrug.

"Can I just say one thing?" He looks me dead in the eye. "You are fabulous."

And he means it. I can tell. He means it, and I'm so thrilled to be around someone who thinks I'm fabulous, I actually start giggling. We order our food. Caroline and I go for the most expensive stuff on the menu, but Vaughn orders a salad, and we commend him on his strength and fortitude in the face of a large, looming expense account. I can feel myself begin to relax. I wonder why I haven't spent more time with Caroline. It's so much fun to be around people who think I'm fabulous. Vaughn is so at ease and he's so good at making us at ease that I think he should be paid for this. Although I don't know in what capacity it would work. . . .

"Parker is the most amazing musician—"

My thoughts are interrupted by Caroline's voice, and I start to say that I really don't feel like getting into my music right now, when she tactfully continues, "But she's taking a break." So I don't have to explain, and the good mood at the table continues. I learn that Vaughn is working on a novel about a woman who's trapped in a loveless marriage. She inherits a home, which she's remodeling, and she falls in love with a ghost who lives in the house. His idea is to do a new spin on the romance genre. He wants it to be a series, with companion home décor books for each novel. Frankly, I think it's genius, and judging by Caroline's nodding head, she does too. He orders another drink and then starts bitching about his day job at a shop on Spring Street. His boss is giving him a hard time because he wants to bring in a new line of handbags from Italy made by a designer who works in plastics.

"You mean Luisa Riedizioni?" I ask, not believing how in sync we are. It's kismet. Vaughn really flips this time, as I tell him about my brief foray into textile design, and how I'm obsessed with textures and shapes. That I can't quite figure it all out, but somehow I think there's a way to assimilate all of these things into my life. And I don't mean through the purchase of a bag. I tell him how I maxed out an entire credit card buying Dorothy Liebes mixed-media woven fabrics, and he nearly falls off his chair. He demands to know how Caroline met me. Caroline, getting drunk, laughs. "Over a shared love of egg-and-cheese sandwiches and a deep-rooted obsession with television characters."

Vaughn rolls his eyes. "Please tell me, Parker. You're not into *La Femme Nikita*?"

"No."

"Good."

"For me it's *MEDS*."

"Sweetie, I'll tell you what I told Caroline. Take a deep breath, count to ten, and say the words 'It's just a show' ten times."

Caroline is cracking up.

"I've tried that, it doesn't work. I can't imagine life without him."

"I understand, Parker, but you have to quash it, or it takes you over. Like me and *Wallpaper* magazine. I had to stop reading it. It was showing me a life I could never attain." He drains his glass. "I lived for the next issue, and then it would come, and I'd have this outrageous high for a few days, but the reality that it would never be my life would plunge me into a deep funk for weeks afterward." He pours himself another drink and pauses dramatically. "So I *canceled* my subscription and never looked at it again."

I'm not buying it. He's too amazingly fun to be so well adjusted. "You're full of shit," I say with a burst of insight. "You sneak it! You look at it on the stand, but you don't buy it."

He cracks up laughing. Busted. "It doesn't count if I don't buy it!"

We all nod our heads.

"Well, for me, the thing with M . . . it's taken on a life of its own." I lean in, not for effect but because I haven't admitted this to anyone. "I love him."

Vaughn looks at me. Then at Caroline, who just nods her head because she understands.

"Sweetie, you need help. I told Caroline the same thing when she went through the whole Nikita and Michael trauma. You need to get out of the house, you need to mingle, and you need to stop watching TV. It's that simple. You're depressed; that's all this is. Come down to the store;

I've got a vat of Paxil. We can nip this in the bud. I've got some Riedizioni samples; I'll give you a few."

Caroline pays the bill and leaves a big tip at my urging. I look at my watch. It's just after three. I'm supposed to be at the diner on Christopher Street in fifteen minutes. This is working out perfectly. We all head out together and stand in front of the restaurant for a moment, promising to do this another time soon. Then Caroline brings up my music again, because she's just remembered Vaughn's boyfriend owns a club in Tribeca. She was at the café that infamous night. She never saw me dressed in black playing Bach; she only sees me in the Ludlow light. I'm grateful. I realize that for once, someone has the right impression of me. Vaughn says the club is a sort of work-in-progress, for people who are a work-in-progress. And suddenly I find myself getting excited; I could have a venue, with a group of like-minded people—textile obsessed, texturally challenged, pathologically lying, television-obsessed people such as myself.

"When you're done with this creative hiatus of yours, call me. I'll introduce you to my boyfriend. He'll *love* you."

I throw my arms around him and really think he could be my new best friend. I look at my watch again. It's twenty after. As I walk quickly up the street, I shut all good thoughts out of my mind. I have only one goal now: to free Lil. I will free Lil, and then I will plot my musical return, which will pick up from where I left off in the basement of the Ludlow Street Café. As if everything in between was a mere glitch.

I'll play at Vaughn's boyfriend's club, and my life will

begin. I'll be fabulous on a very large level, and M will come to the club, and he will see that I am a genius, and he will fall in love with me, and we will live together. And I will pay down my credit-card debt. Life will be good, and I will no longer feel the compulsive need to be a liar. I will reference my early years in interviews, when I struggled to define myself and my art, and I will tell people that I was a liar, but it will seem artistic and necessary; merely my artistic impulse gone awry, a manifestation of a deep-seated desire to express myself. My father will read about me in the *New York Times*, and he will regret disowning me. I will, of course, refuse any of his attempts to contact me, and the media will ponder the nature of the feud.

All this as I head into the diner. It's three-thirty on the dot. The phone rings, and I remind myself that I am now in character.

"Are you alone?"

"If you mean does anyone else know about this, then yes, I am alone. If you mean am I alone in the diner, the answer is no. I'm surrounded." I'm decidedly flip. I'm sure Nikita would approve.

"Shut up! Just have the money by four, and bring it to the south side of the Christopher Street station, then throw it onto the center track."

If I'm to throw it onto the center track, I wonder, why do I have to enter on the south side? Then I get confused, because there is no south side. There is only an east and a west side. Or maybe not. I don't know. "Throw the money onto the *center* track?"

"That's what we said! Throw it on the track and step away. She'll come out of the next passing southbound train."

They're confusing south with downtown. The line goes dead, but I know what I'm supposed to do. I call the number that Mr. Smith gave me. A gruff voice answers.

"Yes."

I'm thrown off by this. I don't know who I'm talking to; I don't know how much they know. It's decidedly awkward. "Ah, *yeah,* this is Parker Grey. . . . I'm calling about . . . the *situation.* . . . I don't know if I'm supposed to say more but—"

"Where do you need it and when?"

This makes things much easier. "I need it at the Christopher Street station by four o'clock."

"I will meet you at Gay Street in twenty minutes."

"That's cutting it a little close."

"Gay Street, twenty minutes. You walk fast, you'll make the drop-off."

The Pillpopper and I once looked at a co-op on Gay Street. I loved it, but being the homophobe that he was, Dana refused to live there. I should've left him then. I stand on the corner of Gay and Bleecker, looking around for a sign. I see an ominous black BMW pull onto the street. Sure enough, the window pulls down, and a shiny silver suitcase is passed out to me. I'm suddenly extremely paranoid; this feels like a drug deal.

"You have five minutes. Go."

I'm on autopilot. I take the case and start walking. Fast. Well, as fast as I can, considering the case weighs a ton.

Christ, I've got *two million dollars*. I turn back and see that the BMW is following me, tailing me, and I find this a relief. At least someone's got my back. I head down into the train station, buy my token, and I'm in. It occurs to me that throwing a suitcase onto the express tracks without anyone noticing may not be so simple. Worse still, what if I hit the third rail and the thing explodes? My heart pounds as I walk to the end of the platform. I tell myself to focus. I wish I had a soundtrack to calm my nerves. I've kept music out of my head for so long now, all I can come up with is the theme from *Shaft*. When it gets to the part about the dick getting all the chicks, it just doesn't work, and I reach the end of the platform not calm, cool, or collected, like Nikita. No, I'm a circus freak, muttering to myself and sweating. I look around and hurl the money fast.

It falls straight down onto the local track.

I wonder why it is never easy. I don't know how they expected me to hurl it across the track, which when I look at it, is about twenty feet. It's not like I'm a shot-putter, and the thing weighs a ton. And now I've got a problem. The case is not in the proper place. If I don't move it, it's going to get run over, and things will turn out, for lack of a better word, badly. I've got no choice. I have to jump down onto the tracks. I tell myself that kids do it all the time and that surely it can't be as terrifyingly dangerous as the Transit Authority would have us believe. I jump.

Immediately it's a bad idea. Like something out of Kafka, there are two big monstrous lights coming at me in the distance. I freeze. I am going to die. I think about my funeral. It should be a big one because I'm young. Then again, a closed casket always makes for a smaller show. I wonder what my mother will put me in. My mother has no fashion sense and even less when it comes to fabrics. I see myself in my pink organdy prom dress from high school. The one we bought in the back room at Loehmann's. I unfreeze and choose life.

I grab the case and dive into the middle track as the train passes. It's not as terrifying as I would have thought because the train slows down and stops. I dump the case in the center track, step over the third rail—which *is* terrifying—and climb back up on the small staircase at the end of the platform that I failed to see before. The train screeches off just as another one enters the station.

Suddenly there's a lot of commotion and noise, and there are people everywhere. I run toward the head of the platform. *Where is Lil?* I jump into the open door of the downtown train. Through the window. I see a figure on the tracks. He's got the case. The bell rings, a major third interval, I note, and I dive off the train. Back onto the platform. The train pulls away, and the express train cruises past, and I'm running back and forth, searching through the faces of the people who are getting off the train and heading up the stairs, and I'm yelling Lil's name. Suddenly I'm terrified.

This isn't a show.

This is real, and she should be here.

I had imagined that we'd hug, and I'd tell her all about M, and we'd have a drink and a laugh, and she'd break it off with Smith, and we'd tell this story to our children when we were old ladies. I thought that we'd look back on this thing as a madcap adventure. We'd chalk it up to inexperience and youth. We'd chalk it up . . .

I stand in one spot, looking behind me, ahead of me, all around me. But the place has cleared out, and now there's only me and some tired-looking woman who's just taken a seat on the bench. She's reading the *Christian Science Monitor*.

And Lil is nowhere to be found.

TWELVE

I hit the ground running. I'm barely through the apartment door, and the phone is ringing. The machine picks up before I can reach it.

"Hey Parker, Tom Humphrey calling. Listen, I heard through the grapevine that you're no longer playing, and it's always been my policy that my guitars must be played, so I'd appreciate it if you'd give me a call so we could discuss the possibility of me buying back the guitar. If you remember, we discussed this when you first purchased it. . . . Thanks much. . . ."

With everything that's going on, why does Tom have to call *now*? I didn't want him to know I quit. This means I will be forced to either lie or sell Humphrey back at a serious cut rate. I signed a paper authorizing this. I can't believe that everything is going so *wrong*. My thoughts are racing fast; I don't know what to do next. Then the phone rings again. I jump to answer it.

"Is this some kind of fucking joke?"

The voice is angry, hostile. I recognize it immediately. "You didn't let her go!"

"There was *no fucking money* in the suitcase."

And my mind starts spinning even faster. That's impossible, unless when I dropped it, the money fell out on the tracks? But I would've seen that. How could there be no money? The man in the black BMW assured me that the money was there. He told me to walk to the station, that he'd watch me. *Impossible.* It was all there. The case weighed a ton. How could it have been empty? They're lying. This is some ruse to get more money out of us. I say *us* as if it's my money.

"The *money* was there, but where was *she*?"

"Get us the money or she's dead."

The line goes silent, and I realize that I'm in way over my head. I'm in too deep, and I can't deal with this. This is bad. Bad. My thoughts are racing out of control, and I can hardly catch up to them. I just can't deal.

And the colored paper is just sitting there. I stop thinking. And then I paste paper onto the wall. One color after another. I seem to know which one should come next as if by instinct. The red, then the yellow, followed by three greens, and then a brown to a blue. Back to red, moving down to pink, I just keep going, one sheet after another. The white wall is disappearing beneath a string of color. And with it, so do I.

The calm takes over. I am returning to character, and we

are back from our commercial break. *The Parker Grey Show,* starring Parker Grey. And everyone knows that Parker Grey is cool, calm, fearless. She is the hero. She knows what to do.

Call Smith. Parker would call Smith

I pull out the scrap of paper in my pocket purse and find Smith's number. His secretary answers, and I ask for him.

"And this is regarding?"

The kidnapping of his lover. I consider saying it, but don't. "He'll know what it's regarding." I wait for what seems to be an eternity. The canned music comes in, another obscure guitar concerto. Telemann. I eyeball Humphrey. He really needs to get over himself.

"I'm sorry, he doesn't know what this is regarding. He's a busy man. Please don't call again."

She hangs up.

And there it is. Smith didn't put any money in the case. But I stay calm because I'm certain there's a way out of this. I think about the last call from the kidnappers. And I remember something. I go into Lil's room. An explosion of books and papers. I rummage through the mess, looking for her big, fancy phone. It's very slick, lots of buttons including a caller ID readout on the top. I push a button, and it shows me the last number that called. I pick up the phone and dial. It's a cell phone, and it's off. The person isn't reachable. Could they be this stupid? I call information. I tell them the number.

"That's a cell phone. There's a name on it, but I can't give it to you."

"Why not?"

"Invasion of privacy. I'd tell you, but these calls are recorded, and I could get in trouble with my supervisor."

"But I don't need a name, I need an address."

"There's only a billing address, and the number is blocked."

I hang up. Undeterred. There has to be a way. Lil's computer. I get on-line and start searching. I've never spent much time on the Internet. I never had time to spend on anything but music. I find a search engine and put in the number. I don't know what I'm looking for, but I'm confident. I'm the hero; I have to find it. I'm given a dozen different sites that deal with phone numbers and retrieval. I click on one. And in the top right corner, another window opens up.

An ad for *MEDS*.

I think this must be a sign.

Perhaps M is telling me to be strong. Or letting me know that he's always with me. Against my better judgment, I click on it. Another window comes up. It's some site devoted to the show. I tell myself to find the name first, and then as a reward I can go back and look. I continue to search, finding my way through the maze rather well. I find a site, I punch in the number, and I am given an address: 490 Elizabeth Street, Apt. 4F. Armed with the address, I go for my reward.

I double-click the *MEDS* site. I see a photo of M looking amazingly good. I click on it, and it takes me to an unofficial fan site. I click again, and I'm in a ring, a Web ring that has hundreds of fan sites, all devoted to M. This is sort of troubling. I'm appalled that all these people seem to think that they have a connection to M. For the first time I realize I am not the only one thinking about him day and night. And now a larger question looms. Am I a pathetic fan?

Screw M and all his little groupies! I have no time for idiocy! I have my own lives to save! I pull on the sexiest skirt I have. Dolce & Gabbana, floral. Loehmann's. It's last year's but it fits perfectly. I find a bottle of pepper spray in Lil's room. I don't think she's ever used it. She just likes the idea of it. A strappy halter number and a pair slingbacks, and I'm out the door. I'm going to do this in style. I think Nikita would be proud.

Three blocks into my trek, I realize that the heels were a mistake. And the thong panties are riding my crack. There are people everywhere, so reaching up to pull them out is just not an option. It's very hard to be a cool, save-the-world chick when all you can think about is a thong ribbon riding your ass and how badly you're dying to put on a pair of flat shoes. I curse myself for getting caught up in the moment.

Four ninety Elizabeth Street. The name on the buzzer for 4F is Colin Richards. Colin Richards. It sounds like a kidnapper's name. I'm not sure how to proceed, but there's a delivery guy going in. I follow him.

The delivery guy takes the elevator. I take the steps. Four flights in the heels, and I'm winded. I either have to quit smoking or start exercising, although neither seems like a viable option. Four F is the last apartment in the hallway. I creep toward the door, pulling out the pepper spray in the process. It's got some kind of safety top on it that makes it look like a grenade, and I can't get the damn thing off. I approach the door slowly and peek my eye into the peephole. I can see nothing. Suddenly the door swings open. I jump out of the way. A tall blonde comes walking out with some guy who I presume to be Colin. In a desperate attempt to appear casual, I pretend to knock on an adjacent door, while sticking the can of pepper spray into my armpit. But they don't even notice me.

"What the fuck, Colin? That was a really nice Treo."

"It's just a phone; I'll get another."

"I gave that to you for your birthday. . . ."

My heart sinks. Colin Richards lost his Treo phone, and I know who has it. Now what?

I head back downstairs. I take the steps again and pass Colin and his girlfriend on the way out. He holds the door open for me, leaving his girlfriend standing on the sidewalk waiting for him. As I pass through the doorway, she looks at me. And we have an entire conversation without words.

He's never going to change.

I can change him.

No, you can't. Trust me on this one.

They head off in the opposite direction. I'm back to square one. The only thing I know now is that the kidnappers have a cellular phone, and that they stole it from Colin Richards. I begin to think once again that I should call the police. The more I walk, the more abundantly clear this becomes.

I will go home. I will call the police. I will do that.

I head up Greenwich Street, but my knees are shaking and my nerves are shot. My feet are killing me, and my ass is rubbed raw. I need to rest. I need to smoke. Just for five minutes. And the bar is right here. I sit down outside. Laurel and Margaret are arguing about *Iron Chef*.

"Iron Chef Japanese, he's so fucking smug. He plays it like he's all humble, but he's always mentioning Robert De Niro. He's a star fucker. I hate him."

Margaret hates everyone. Laurel's more matter-of-fact about it all.

"He's all right."

I watch *Iron Chef,* but only because there's nothing else on during its time slot. The dubbing is really what makes the show, all those literal translations. There's always some petite Japanese actress saying things like, "I like the way it feels on my tongue and as it rolls down my throat I have the sensation of springtime in Kyoto." I pull a smoke out of Laurel's pack, which is sitting in her apron pocket. I don't even bother to say hello. There's really no need. The bar is open practically twenty hours a day, and like the beer, it's a free flow. One minute you're working, the next you're not, but you can stop by, interrupt someone else's conversation, bum a smoke, have a small glass of beer, and then leave. It's like a cheap date just around the corner. I add my two cents to the conversation. "I think it would be more interesting if the losing chef had to perform ritual hara-kiri in front of the studio audience."

Margaret sparks to the notion. "Now *that* I would watch."

Esme drops a tray of beers over on table five and joins us. I've forgiven her for flirting with M, and I share my smoke with her. "What was the ingredient last night?"

"It was boring, mushrooms. . . ." Esme takes a closer look at me "*Jes*us Parker . . . what's up with the pepper spray?

"Uhhh . . . protection." I'd forgotten I was holding it.

"Protection against what?"

I shouldn't be telling any of this, but I feel the need to unburden myself. And so I do. In small increments of half
truths. "This guy's been calling my apartment and . . ." Half
truth. ". . . hanging up. So I got the number, and I found out
his address, and I went over there."

Laurel looks at me like I'm insane. "Is he calling like a hundred times a day?"

"No. Just like six times."

"What were you gonna do?"

I was going to save my friend who was kidnapped. "I was
gonna tell him to stop fucking calling."

They're all laughing as Esme tries to comprehend what I'm
telling her. "You were gonna ring his bell, he answers the
door . . . you shout, 'Don't call my house *fucker*!!' and then
you *spray* him?"

Even I'm cracking up now, because when she tells it that
way, it *is* pretty funny. Margaret is the only one who remains
serious. "She had no choice. When someone violates you, you
have to take things into your own hands. . . ."

Laurel rolls her eyes. "Lighten up, Mags."

"But it turned out he wasn't the guy. It was his cell phone,
but someone stole it from him. They're the ones calling my
apartment."

Now Esme's confused. "Who?"

"The ones who stole the phone . . ."

Laurel takes my smoke to light her own. "Parker . . . You
are so whacked."

And I feel the pang of guilt. We're here together, bonding,
doing what friends do. But I'm lying to them, which makes

this all completely false. Esme puts her arm around my shoulder. "I love you, Parker . . . You're such an original."

If she only knew. I lie to them, and they're so nice to me. It's too much. I feel like I could cry. Esme looks at me. "You okay, Parker . . . ?"

Not really. "Yeah . . . I'm fine."

Cigarettes are extinguished, and Esme, Laurel, and Margaret go back to work.

I go home.

THIRTEEN

In my underwear, sipping a cold bottled water from the fridge, holding a notepad, staring at the plasma screen, totally avoiding. *Dark Eyes* is on Bravo. Marcello Mastroianni is telling his sad story of regret to a woman whose face is obscured by a giant hat. He tells her how he married for money and lost the woman he truly loved. But the woman in the hat *is* the woman he loved. It's a gorgeous, sweeping epic. Everything that my life is not.

It's time to bite the bullet.

Smith has screwed Lil and by proxy me, and now there's only one choice. Which is to call the police, who should've been called in the first place. I have to do it. I know this. I *don't* know how to begin, so I have jotted down what I'm going to say. This works for socially challenged people such as myself. "Hello, I'm calling because my friend was kidnapped." I will start there. I pick up the phone and dial the First Precinct.

"If this is a life-threatening emergency please push One. All other calls please hold."

I've gotten a prerecorded message. Unbelievable. I can't bring myself to push One because I'm uncertain about the definition of "life-threatening." What if I tie up the line and someone's having a heart attack and they can't get to them because of me? I think the technical term is *involuntary manslaughter*. Instead, I stay on the line. I'm told that a representative will be with me shortly. And so I wait. My brain churning in anticipation.

The police will want to know where she was kidnapped, and odds are Smith is going to deny that she was in his home. But they can do DNA tests and verify that she was there. Which means they'll be able to verify that I was there too. They'll wonder about that. They'll think it's all some setup. They'll ask about the confidentiality agreement I signed for Smith. Then they'll search the apartment. They'll ask about the plasma screen. There will be a torrent of questions, and I won't have the right answers. Beads of sweat forming. My face is getting hot. They're not going to believe me. I'm going to sound like a freak. And if the kidnappers find out I went to the cops, they'll kill Lil, and Smith is going to deny all involvement, and the bad guys will win, and my show will be panned by the critics for all of eternity. I see myself in jail having sex with guards for cigarettes.

"First Precinct. Can I help you?"

I slam the phone down. And no sooner do I hang up than it rings. The police have star-69ed me! Now I'm in deep shit. They *know* I've called! I'm trapped; I've got no choice but to pick up.

"Hello . . ."

"Fucking asshole stiffed me."

It's Lil! A rush of adrenaline surges through my body. "Lil?! Are you okay?! Where are you?!" But she's not listening. She's upset.

"My own *father*! He doesn't give a *shit*! *Daddy can't even come through for me!*"

I suspect they're only feeding her carbohydrates. This is a common tactic among kidnappers and cult leaders because starchy foods make you dopey and affect your ability to reason. Lil's irrational speech is probably a direct result of this. "Tell me where you are! Can you talk? Are they there? Where are you?"

"They're going to give you six days—"

"Six days?"

"Six days to get the money! My *own father* . . ."

Lil is sublimating her suppressed anger for her father onto Smith. She has had no protein in days. She is losing it. "Lil, he's *not* your father. Smith *isn't* your father. You have to—"

She cuts me off. *"It's all down on paper. . . ."*

She whispers this. An urgent, almost guttural whisper. I have no clue what she's talking about but I know I'm supposed to. I have no idea how much time I have, or for that matter how much time she has before they take the phone away from her.

"Lil, I don't know *what to do*!" I'm shouting now. "Where am I going to get the money? Smith's ignoring me! Where are you?! Are you okay? Should I call the cops?"

"*No!* Don't do that! Just get the money—"

And the line goes dead.

I hurl the phone across the floor, it lands with a thud next to Humphrey. "It's all down on paper." What the hell does that *mean? All down on paper.* Why did she say that? I look up at the colored papers on the wall. All on paper. I look at the movie. Marcello's leaving a note for his lover, but she never gets it. *All down on paper . . .*

★

I tear through Lil's room. I find dirty socks, old photos, matchbooks from places that aren't even open anymore. Jars of pennies, letters from old friends, a box of hair. I don't want to know what that's all about. Then under the bed, I find wisdom teeth jammed into a voodoo doll. I recall vaguely that Lil had given her teeth to a boyfriend, as a "gesture." Her word, not mine. When they broke up, he returned the teeth with the voodoo doll and then he stalked her for a month before she had to get a restraining order against him.

Finally, deep under the bed, I grab a red lacquer box buried under a pile of sweaters. Lil's version of summer storage. I pull it out and open it. And it's the jackpot. A giant pile of love letters from Smith. Who knew he was such the romantic? I read through a few of the letters. He's fond of quoting Shelley and Byron, although I'm not impressed, and I'm certain Lil wasn't either. She's penciled in the margins on a few of them little notes like, "What a cliché" and "Get the quote right if you're going to use it." There must be at least forty of them. All on engraved personal stationery, all addressed "To my beautiful Lil," and all signed, "I love you with all my heart." Clearly, these love letters are not something that Smith wants circulated. Especially since his wife had him put everything and the kitchen sink in her name.

I pile up the letters and shove them into an envelope. Yes, these will not go over well with the wife. This is exactly how I will get Smith to give me Lil's ransom money. And since he dragged my ass into this, and because he is a complete coward, I decide to add a thirty-three thousand–dollar fee to the bill.

Thirty-three thousand is my credit-card debt. It means nothing to him, and it will mean everything to me. I'm certain Lil would want it this way.

FOURTEEN

Kinko's is a strange place, populated by odd people obsessed with collation, paper grade, and copier imaging. Strange as they are, I admire their commitment to the process. There's a white guy with dreadlocks and a big Jamaican hat behind the counter. You just know he goes to NYU and he's from Scarsdale and his mother is stroking out because he wears that big hat everywhere he goes. I picture Thanksgiving, with his mom offering him cash bribes to lose the Rasta hat. I buy a copy card, and he looks at me like the amateur that I am. His eyes say it all: *You'll never be able to do it alone. Hand them over.* But I can't. They've got Smith's name on them.

And I am nothing, if not discreet.

I feel the eyes of the white Rasta on me as I place the first incriminating letter into the machine. He's waiting for me to fail, but after a few adjustments, I get it together. Rasta boy is still staring at me, as if to say, *You should've just let me do it.* But I don't acknowledge him. Instead, I turn my attention to a middle-aged guy copying something out of a magazine. He's pasty, as if he hasn't eaten meat in a while, and he's wearing flip-flops. I wonder what his deal is. He looks lonely, but maybe he isn't. Maybe he's got a wife waiting for him at home. Maybe the article is for his kid, or he's a writer and it's his, and he's making copies to send to his mother, so she can see that he did amount to something after all. He doesn't notice me. He's not wondering what I'm copying. There are something like nine million people living in Manhattan. I think how utterly isolated we all are from one another. Nine million people out there, all the stories, all the trials and tribulations, and we can't even look one another in the eye.

★

Midnight, and I'm in the beer cellar of the bar. I slipped in through the back entrance, and no one saw me. I've watched enough TV to know that the original letters must be hidden. The beer cellar seems perfect. Only Peaches goes down there, and Peaches can't read. I hide a packet of the original letters behind an old Schaefer beer sign that's lying in the corner. Up the cellar steps, no sign of Boomer, no sign of anyone. I cruise past the fry cook, who barely notices me, and I'm nearly out the door—

"Parker . . . How the hell are you, hon?"

I turn and see him sitting at a table in the back. My alcoholic boss, last seen screaming to me about responsibility.

"Hey, Tommy." He's never called me hon, so immediately I'm dubious. The Tony Soprano shit-eating grin on his face is cause for even more alarm.

"I heard about your run-in with some of our friends in the blue suits."

I rack my brain trying to recall which lie he might be referencing.

"And at first I'm wondering, what the fuck is she getting involved for?"

I'm still at a loss.

"Cocksuckers come in here twice a year and bug something."

It's the FBI guy lie I told, coming back to bite me in the ass. My lies. They haunt me. And yet, I was in character when I told that one. It wasn't really me.

"But Parker, I nearly pissed myself when I found out that you were fucking with them! What? You have your friend call and goof around about a kidnapping?"

My mouth goes dry. "Kidnapping?"

"You don't have to play dumb with me. They were in here today asking me about it. Of course, I played stupid, but then I remembered what Lenny told me, about how you said you saw the cocksuckers bugging the phone, and I realized that it was you. I laughed my balls off."

He cracks up and then chokes on a wad of phlegm. The phone was bugged! It was *actually* bugged. The good news is, I'm not a liar. The bad news is, the Feds heard me talking to both Smith and the kidnappers. *Stay calm Parker. Stay calm.*

"I was telling my old man about it. I said Parker Grey was

fucking with the Feds during her shift, and then it hits me like a ton of bricks." He narrows his gaze. Leans in, like we're partners in crime. "Big Bill Grey, the Westie. He any relation?"

I hold my tongue on this one. Big Bill Grey, the Westie. Never heard of the guy, but Westies are known for cutting up bodies that the Mafia doesn't want to deal with. I cannot allow myself to say that I'm related to some killer who may or may not still be alive. I can just see me saying he's my uncle, and then Tommy gets him on the horn, and next thing I know, I'm quitting my job and never walking on Spring Street again. My silence is palpable, and Tommy just nods his head.

"I understand. I know how it is with relations. Don't worry, Parker. Your secret's safe with me."

He's taking my silence to mean yes, but I could always argue that I meant no. I guess that's the best I can hope for. "I gotta get going, Tommy."

"What the hell were you doing down there anyway?"

"I had to go down the other night. I dropped my keys."

I yank my keys out of my pocket. It's barely a lie. Practically a fib.

"Well, you're okay with me, Parker. You need anything, you let me know."

★

I'm strangely energized. So energized, in fact, that I've hauled the fifteen-foot adjustable aluminum ladder up from the basement. No small feat, up five flights of steps, but I was determined. And now here it is, sitting in the middle of the kitchen. Looking strangely at home. I find myself sitting on the rungs. It's nice to have a chair for a change. We never sit on the orange sofa. But the ladder is nice. It offers different seats at different heights. I wish I'd thought of it sooner. Humphrey looks jealous. I have pity and wipe a layer of dust off him and check his humidity gauge to make sure he's comfortable. Then I write a note to Smith.

I keep it very simple. I take a copy of one of his love letters and write in bold letters, with the shiny silver Sharpie, **"WE NEED TO TALK."** And then, in smaller letters at the bottom, "Please call." I place this into an envelope marked Personal and Confidential. Then I place that into another envelope, which I assume is the one the secretary will open. Then I fumble around looking for the phone book and call the first messenger service listed. The lady on the other end of the phone sounds annoyed.

"Do you have an account with us?"

"I don't."

"This better not be a drug delivery. Thirty years in this business, the only people who call at one A.M. are drug dealers."

The ad specifically says twenty-four hours a day, yet now I'm a drug dealer. "I just need to get a letter out tonight. I'm going out of town first thing in the morning, and I won't be here for a pickup." The truth is, I could wait. But I'll sleep better knowing when I wake up, he'll already have gotten it. If I'm really lucky, it'll ruin his day.

We finally agree that a messenger will arrive in an hour. I

make use of the time. I have white walls to cover. My paper supply is beginning to dwindle, but I think I have enough to make it. I think the wall will be finished in the next few days. I love looking at it. It's like the Colorforms I had when I was a kid, only giant. I've got the glue stick in my underwear, five pieces of paper in my hand, piles of different colors on each rung. I know that this is a safety violation, right up there with running with scissors. But I don't care. I can't be bothered climbing up and down each time I need a new color. And yet, karmically, it's not acceptable. I reach for a sheet of pale blue on the ninth rung, and I knock the ten sheets above it to the ground. Ten sheets of yellow sail down to the floor. It's all very poetic. The fluttering, rhythmic motion, as it plays off the air. The sound as it sweeps to the floor. The way the air moves around it. Lilting. Lovely.

And I'm instantly reminded of a paper chandelier I once saw. It was a medley of poems written in different languages on fluttering paper squares all impaled on sputniklike prongs. Its energy was so palpable that the slightest change in the air set it moving. I remember staring at it in the store, entranced by the rhythm the words seemed to have. There they were flat on the paper, but every time they moved, it was as if they were dancing. It's the connection I need. The connection between the Colorform wall and the graffiti wall. The colors and the words. There has to be motion to connect them. A paper chandelier would tie it all together.

I realize that I'm losing my mind to this, but I surrender nonetheless.

I use an entire set of Smith's photocopied letters to make it.

Only I don't have sputnik prongs, I have shish kebab spears that I bought a month ago. In the event that we would be shish kebabbing. Luckily, they're very minimalist. They remind me of the motorcycle spoke my brother was supposed to be able to shove through his arm. I'm weaving my lies into the chandelier. As I work, my jaw begins to pound, and I take my pack of smokes and stuff it in my mouth. Anything to alleviate the pain. The pack works well, but I'm salivating onto my T-shirt. Other than that, I'm very content. Just spearing the letters, trying to find symmetry to the arrangement as I thread string through the letters and impale them with the shish kebab spears. I find peace in the rhythmic motion until the buzzer rings.

I pull on a pair of pants and answer the door. The messenger is there, dressed like an alien. I've never actually seen a messenger in full regalia up close. It's one thing when they're speeding past you on Sixth Avenue, in their goggles and colored pants and suspenders and wacky looking hats. It's an entirely different thing when they're standing on your doorstep at two A.M. I can't figure out why he's wearing swimming goggles.

"Holy shit! Parker?!"

He whips off the goggles.

And I realize it's Adam. We went to music school together. I'm going to be trusting *Adam* with this letter. I'm dismayed, but Adam doesn't sense this. He just invites himself in. Adam was always very arrogant but also very talented. I had a big crush on him. He never gave me the time of day. I tried to get into this experimental group he started, but he took one look at me and said, "Fuck this, I don't want a girl in the band." That one comment set me back. It eroded my self-confidence so badly that I spent the entire semester trying to prove to him that I could play. That I was good enough for him. And now he is standing in front of me, dressed like Mork on acid.

"Great crib."

There's nothing worse than a white guy talking black lingo. He's checking out my place, and I find myself wanting to cover up the graffiti wall. It's too personal. I don't want him to see it. But why the sudden paranoia? What do I care what he thinks anymore? He's still looking around. He's going to say something. He's going to say something disparaging about the Bonnie Cashin graffiti wall, and I'm going to go into a tailspin. But instead he looks at the Colorform wall.

"That's cool."

That's all he says. I'm not sure if it's good or bad. It's sort of noncommittal, and since I've been expending a huge amount of energy on it I find myself offended.

"This place is huge."

Square footage is always an awe-inspiring thing in Manhattan, but why hasn't he commented on the graffiti wall? He probably doesn't like it. Screw him. One comment, six years ago, and I'm still looking for his approval.

"How do you afford this place?"

I'm not about to tell him. "I do okay."

"So what have you been up to?"

"This and that." I keep it vague. I'm too tired to make up some elaborate lie. Adam just stands there. Looking around.

My vagueness doesn't seem to bother him. If I were him, I'd want more answers. "And you?"

"I'm getting a band together; we're going to be doing some new stuff. You should come down. We're going to be at The Knitting Factory. You'd dig it."

Presumptuous, arrogant Adam hasn't changed at all. "Maybe." I hand him the envelope. He puts it in his bag. A little too casually for my liking. "You know where that's going, right?"

"Yeah, I know. Can I use your john?"

I nod, sure. He heads in. A couple moments later, he's out, and he leaves.

"Ciao."

I nod my head. *Ciao. Whatever.* Then I poke my head into the bathroom and see that he didn't lift the seat. Closer inspection reveals drops of piss on my toilet. The balls on this guy. He uses my bathroom and doesn't even bother to clean up his own excrement. And then it hits me with absolute clarity: it was never me. Adam is simply a jerk. He's an arrogant jerk. He's no better off than I am, and he never was, but he *thinks* he is. I can't believe I've just spent the last few minutes worrying about what he might say! But I become aware of something else. This time I don't want his approval. I want his arrogance. I wish I had just a piece of it. Maybe then I wouldn't be in the mess I'm in.

I return to my work. I will not allow myself to expend another ounce of energy on the past.

★

Instead, I spend an hour hoisting my chandelier, which looks amazing. Then I watch *High & Low*. Kurosawa. Not one of his historical epics, just a kidnapping story, which, I think, is apt. But it's the blocking that's really interesting. Every scene in the picture is flawless in its composition. If I had an ear like Kurosawa's eye, I might consider playing again. If I could figure out a way to make music visual somehow, I might be tempted.

FIFTEEN

In my dreams that night, I was staring at the Colorform wall, and I swear I could hear music coming from it. For a brief moment I had it all figured out; I merged sight with sound and it was exactly right, but then my brain banked a hard left, and I was living it up in the Hotel California. Humphrey was there, and Joe Walsh was telling me I needed to find God. I tried to leave, but obviously, I was unable to.

★

Smith finally calls at eleven. Early enough to let me know that he's nervous. Late enough to send the message that he's not intimidated.

"You are playing with fire. No one screws with me."

"I believe that you're the one screwing with me. You gave me an empty briefcase." There's silence.

"I don't know what you're talking about."

"Of course you do. I need the money to get Lil."

"I don't know anyone named Lil."

"Not according to the pile of letters I found in her room, written on your personal stationery."

"I'm telling you. I don't know you, I don't know Lil, I don't know anything. That's my story. Good-bye."

He hangs up on me. Just like that. I should be rattled, but I'm not. I have to be at work in twenty minutes, yet somehow I'm completely confident that this is going to work out.

★

The lunch shift is the pits. People don't go out of their way to lunch at a bar that makes greasy burgers and bad salads. As a result, it's only the regulars, the ones who have been coming in for fifty years. They used to come in at night but got too old, and so now they come and drink during the day. There are only two waitresses working, me and Diane, who wants to be an actress. She stays in the back reading. I work the out-door section. The worst part about working lunch is that you know you're not going to make any money until happy hour, and even then, if you don't get paid before the next shift comes on, the check gets carried over to the next waitress, and you're shit out of luck. Normally, I'd be skimming off my bar tabs, but I don't bother. It all seems so pointless, this endless struggle for money. Viola is sitting outside. She's a nice old lady who always has a plain turkey sandwich on white and a

Cosmopolitan. Then she takes her crumbs and feeds the birds.

"I see you have an admirer."

Viola hasn't had a moment of clarity since 1963, so I take her comment in stride.

"At this point I'll take what I can get."

"Well, this one is very handsome. He was just inside staring at you."

My heart races. Could it be M? I rush inside, but the only person sitting there is Benny the Longshoreman. I head back outside, just in time to notice a big black BMW as it skulks past the bar. The windows are tinted and I can't see the driver, but it looks just like Smith's car from the other day, and I have the distinct impression that the person inside the car is looking at me. I give the car the finger. If Smith is indeed sending me a message, I'm sending one right back.

★

Four hours and forty bucks later, I'm back at home. And the place has been totally ransacked. I think about the black BMW drive-by during my shift. And now I am pissed. Smith sent his goons over here to get the letters! And from the looks of it, they searched everywhere. The place is a total wreck, although thankfully they left Humphrey and the Colorform wall alone. I turn on the light in the kitchen and laugh, because hanging above the island, halfway between the Bonnie Cashin graffiti wall and the Colorform wall is my Smith chandelier.

The morons never thought to look up. Smith really needs

to hire better goons. But at least I now know what needs to be done. I grab two photocopied letters off the chandelier. I hate to do it because the balance is really perfect, but Lil's life is on the line. I dig through my closet until I find a great black ensemble. Very formfitting, very Catwoman. I even go commando, because at this point, visible panty line would completely blow my groove.

SIXTEEN

"I'm here to see Karl Malden."

The doorman smiles at me. "I remember you. . . . You were here the other day."

I raise my eyebrow. "Yes, I was."

He leans in. "The wife is home."

"I know; he likes it that way."

From the look on his face, the doorman has just achieved penile erection. And while I understand that the notion of two women together in a sexual way is titillating, is the thought of me and Mrs. Smith together really all that erotic? It doesn't matter. He lets me up in the private elevator.

★

I stop in the party entrance and make my way out onto the patio. I creep up the stone steps until I reach the wraparound terrace that runs its way around the entire perimeter of the apartment. It's dark and no one can see me, but still I feel the need to crawl. I think of Caroline. She would so love to be here, but I can't risk involving her. After all, this is not a game.

I make it around the eastern section of the terrace and turn the corner. There's a light coming from within a room. I peer in and see it's Smith's bedroom. Mrs. Smith is there; she's wearing some sort of long, flowing nightgown, which probably gets all bunched up when she sleeps. Nightgowns seem like a good idea, but you always wake up with them around your neck. Smith comes out. He's in boxers and a T-shirt. He looks decidedly old. I almost take pity on him. He's heading toward the French doors. He opens them.

"Close that door!"

"I need some air."

"Turn up the humidifier."

He shuts the door but doesn't lock it. Perfect. I wait for him to walk out of the room, and then I creep inside and am overwhelmed with the scent of gardenias. I remember Lil telling me that his wife spends four thousand dollars a week on fresh-cut flowers. Each night before bed, the servants have to put them in the bathtub to soak. Then they revase them before she wakes up in the morning. And the carpet! I've never felt pile like it before. It's like walking on fur. There is no sound. I am Bruce Lee tiptoeing through the opium den in *Enter the Dragon*. I am sleek and cool and confident. I am the hero. If M could see me now, he would fall for me on the spot.

I place the letters on her pillow. I realize this is mean, but so is leaving Lil to die. I slip back out and wait quietly on the terrace as Smith walks back into the room. I'm watching him, but he can't see me. He gets into bed and sees the letters on the pillow next to him. He swipes them away, furious, his face a shock of red. He's heading for the door, but I'm not moving. He's almost to me, but I'm hidden in the inky black of night. He's coming. If he opens the door, I will scream. Almost there. His hand on the knob.

"I told you to *keep that door shut*!"

Smith stands at the door. He knows I'm watching him from the other side of the glass, but he's too pussy-whipped to do anything about it.

"I was just locking it."

And that's when I know. Smith will pay. And not because Smith doesn't want to lose his money, although I'm sure this plays a role. Smith will pay because he's afraid of his wife.

SEVENTEEN

It's hard being the star of the show. Everyone expects so much, and no one really knows the real you. It's a lonely business indeed. Post-Smith, I find myself wandering through the city feeling very alone. I've had too much rush for one day. I'm drained and tired. I think about the final episode of *MEDS*, the way M looked when that nurse dumped him. That's exactly how I feel now. All alone. So I head to the Marriott for a therapy session with Trudy.

I like Trudy because whenever I see her, I can launch into my litany of complaints and she never seems to mind. We met through a bartender at work named John. The same one who was performing air guitar. It was right after I split up with Dana. I was in a bad way, and he was cute, so I had this weird flirtation thing with him that involved the purchase of some very sexy Cosabella underwear. Trudy was always hanging out at the bar, and we became friendly. What I didn't know was that she was his girlfriend. It was sort of a shocker. I was on the verge of blurting out how much I wanted to sleep with him when she started telling me how much she loved him and how they'd been together for eight months. You would never have known they were dating. On more than one occasion I saw him go home with girls from the bar. I really hate infidelity. My father was a big cheat.

Trudy's a career waitress. She doesn't dream of anything else. I think she might be happier if she at least had something to *dream* about, but she doesn't. Trudy's Greek, her dad ran a hot dog stand on Coney Island. So, all things considered, she's doing well. I mean, at least she earns a decent living and has her own apartment.

★

The bar at the Marriott is on the top floor. It's a great view, but the floor rotates. I can't tell if I'm moving or if the windows are moving, and for a moment I think I might get vertigo. I see Trudy, in her skimpy cocktail waitress uniform, carrying a large tray of Pina Coladas, the Midwesterner's martini. She drops the drinks off to a table of chubby businessmen. They say something to her and crack up. There's a lot of knee slapping and belly movement. She puts on her best phony smile, the one she likes to refer to as her "Marriott Smile," and pulls out a laugh from deep inside.

I think working here is bad for her soul.

She is happy to see me. "Thank Marriott! A familiar face!"

Trudy attends Marriott seminars that focus on building team morale. They actually encourage employees to use the word *Marriott* as often as possible.

"Sit your Marriott ass down, and I'll get you a drink." Suddenly Trudy is moving away from me; she's growing smaller by the second. The rotating floor is sucking me into the Marriott vortex. Trudy grabs me before I get swept away. "The floor's a little tricky. Just stay on the carpeted area, and you'll be okay. I'm gonna take a break, get us something to drink."

I sit down. The lounge band is playing "It Never Rains in California." Which is strange because it was the first song I learned how to play. I remember sitting on my parents' bed, the guitar nearly as big as me. And my father moving my fingers into position. Teaching me the different chords.

"It never rains in California . . ."

I remember the pink shag rug in my bedroom, an orange robe, the swing in the backyard. I remember sitting in the grass with my father; he had just had his hair straightened. He wore aviator sunglasses, and there was a black hair sticking out of his nose. He seemed distracted.

"But man I gotta warn you . . ."

After he left, my mother used to sit in the car in the garage and cry. Then she stopped crying, but things were never the same in our house. And the only time I ever felt good was when I was playing my guitar. It passed the hours so peacefully. Just one note in front of the other, just pure mechanics. Move a finger, pluck a string, and sequence one note after another.

"Red wine. A beautiful full-bodied cabernet. Robert Parker gives it a ninety-five."

Trudy returns with wine.

"A Diet Coke would've been fine, and who's Robert Parker?"

She sits down with me. Grabs a smoke from my pack. "You're going to meet someone, and he's going to take you to a nice restaurant, you're not going to order a Diet Coke."

She has a point. I drink the wine. Not so sure that I like it.

"You should taste cherry and oak."

Trudy is taking a wine-tasting class in an attempt to meet a rich man. "What does oak taste like?"

"I don't know, woody."

She knew another woman who did this who ended up marrying some VP over at Lancôme. He has two daughters from a previous marriage who have emotional problems. One thinks she's a lesbian, and the other is screwing her gym teacher. In addition, she had to convert and become Jewish, and this killed her Irish-Catholic grandmother, literally. The old woman had a heart attack a week before the wedding. So I wonder, was it worth it?

"Robert Parker is the premier wine critic in the world. Smell it first, then sip and suck in air with it."

I do as I'm told. "It tastes like sweaty feet."

Trudy laughs. "I think so too! Apparently it's an acquired taste."

"I'll keep trying."

"I'm so happy to see you; I was worried about you. I think you're lonely."

"I am. Horribly."

Trudy considers my loneliness as I consider her hairy eye-brow. Lil would say that this is indicative of larger hair issues. Lil hates body hair. She's always on a quest to rid herself of it. She'll spend hours shaving, plucking, waxing. She always says in her next life, she wants to be Asian. I don't have hair issues, but I am eyebrow obsessed, because eyebrows make the face. Which is why I can't take my eyes off of Trudy's furry brow. I often wonder why she doesn't go to my Brazilian guy and have it plucked. Meanwhile, she's come to a conclusion re-garding my chronic loneliness.

". . . totally common for children of divorce. It stems from fear of abandonment issues—"

"So what's the solution?"

"Just be aware of it. Be aware of your feelings, and always ask yourself where they're coming from. Always try to get to the root. Like you think it's your asshole boss or something, but it's not. That's just a trigger. You have to forget the trig-gers and go to the source. Then you can relive the trauma, as an adult, and get past it . . . ."

Trudy expects so much of me. And yet, something about her always compels me to honesty. "Trudy. I'm in love."

"Get out!? Who!?"

"He's an actor on TV."

"Nice, where'd you meet him?"

"I haven't. But he's come into the bar a few times. . . ."

"And?"

"And nothing."

"So you're a fan."

"No, not a fan." *Definitely not a fan.* "I love him. I really,

really love him." I feel like Sally Field at the Oscars. "I know that I love him, and I've never been more certain about anything in my life."

She's trying real hard to be supportive, but it's tough. "But . . . you don't actually know him?"

"That is correct."

She considers it for a moment. "It's not your usual MO, so maybe there's something to it."

"Trudy, I know I've never spoken to him per se . . ."

"*Per se.*"

I want so very much for her to understand. "But the thing is, I see something in him, I can see the person behind the character, it's like I see behind his mask. . . ."

Trudy looks freaked out. "Holy fuck! I can't believe you just said that. I've been reading this book about how we all wear masks and how we never let them down and how true love is *seeing behind the mask.*"

"Is that by the same person who wrote about the mirroring thing?"

"No. Mirrors are out. Masks are in. It's all about masks. Modern society has forced us to all hide our true selves. You see behind the mask?"

"I do."

"Fucking incredible."

And in that moment I am validated.

"You can't fuck this up."

"There's nothing *to* fuck up."

But Trudy isn't joking. "Let me tell you something, Parker. You're self-destructive."

"You think?"

"Yes. I've never told you that, but I've thought it. You don't do drugs or cut yourself, but you make incredibly stupid choices. Especially when it comes to men. You let them do all the destruction; you allow yourself to be victimized. But if you can see behind his mask, you have a chance for something that's good. It'll be something that's better than anything you've ever had before. But you have to ask yourself: Do I really want to be happy? Can I handle happiness?"

I'm not so certain. I've always been so comfortable wallowing in my general cynical malaise. "Would I be perky all the time?"

"No! You wouldn't lose your edge; you just wouldn't be depressed all the time. You would feel . . ." Trudy searches for the right word. "Content."

I consider contentment. I'm not sure I know what it means. And yet somehow, I think I want in.

EIGHTEEN

I leave the Marriott with a slight buzz. I ride down the elevator with two women dressed in matching purple dresses. They're not much older than me, and they're definitely not from New York. We exchange a glance and then go back to our own little bubbles. In my bubble, I'm thinking that maybe loving M isn't the strangest thing that could happen. People meet in all different ways. The next time M comes into the bar, *if* he comes in, I will speak to him. I will meet him. I hope I'm not too late. The purple duo gets off on the third floor. I will never see them again. The randomness of life confounds me at every turn. From the moment we're conceived to the moment we die, everything is random. It's all left to chance. Yes, if I see M again, I will speak to him. I wasn't ready before. But now I am. In the meantime, I will finish my

Colorform wall. I will continue to put one color in front of the other, just like I'm walking now with one foot in front of the other, until I get home.

★

But my feet find their way into Colony Records instead. For the first time in at least six months, I have the urge to hear a song. It's an old Stevie Wonder tune. I can't remember the name, only the melody. I sort through a bin searching for it. I'll know it when I see it. I hocked my CD collection when I left Dana. I just sold everything. I threw out anything that I didn't have an immediate need for. I even sold my clothes, leaving pieces of myself scattered in secondhand clothing stores. I have no regrets; it was something that had to be done. And I find it. "I Never Thought You'd Leave in Summer." That's the song.

★

Back at home, CD in hand, I remember that I hocked my CD player too. But the DVD player takes CDs. It's strange hearing music in the apartment. It's even stranger hearing it come out of the plasma screen. Lil respected my moratorium on music and hasn't played a thing since I moved in. Now I feel like the walls are buzzing, and Stevie's voice is bouncing all over the apartment. The force is causing Smith's chandelier to spin around, the soft white paper billowing as it dances to his clear voice. And I'm filled with pure, unadulterated glee. The place is still trashed, but now I don't care. I've got Stevie. I have my Colorform wall. I've got my words. And Humphrey too. I have Humphrey.

I pull off my clothes, open all the windows to air the place out a bit, and then I get to work. Even before the goons trashed us, I had let the place go. Now I'm going to put it back together. I scrub the kitchen. Clean all the dishes and put them away. I do laundry, I scrub the floor, I actually change the sheet on my bed, which I haven't slept in for weeks, preferring the window seat. I put everything away. I reorganize, reclaiming all the drawers and closets. As if I'm acknowledging for the first time that this is in fact my home. When I'm done, I climb the ladder and work on the Color-form wall. I'm determined to finish. I need closure. Completion. And so, I work without thought, just placing one color in front of the next.

Five hours later, the wall is finished. I eyeball Humphrey in the corner and pull him over for a look. From the window seat we stare at all the colors hanging there in suspended motion like a giant, living, breathing entity. Full-toned, rich, brilliant.

It's pure harmony.

The graffiti wall is still evolving. The narrative of my strange, brutish life scrawled across the support beam. Like hieroglyphics in some futuristic tomb. I suspect this will always be the case. It will never be completed, but I find solace in this. The narrative of my life is far from over. I read the words, not in any particular order, my eyes bouncing around. Until they reach the top of the beam, where scrawled in red ink I read my own words from this morning. **"In a dream you saw a way to survive."**

And maybe I have found a way to survive. I turn my focus

to Humphrey. There's the hint of a gesture in my motion, and in the gesture, the possibility of a truce. I don't know that I can play again, but I think that maybe I can figure all of this out. Somehow, maybe, I'll be able to find my way out of this tunnel. A way back to myself. Back to the source, like Trudy said.

I reach for Humphrey but stop short of touching him. I can't promise anything. All I can offer him is my empty hand. I feel forgiven, and all at once, for maybe a brief flash, I feel what it is to truly love.

NINETEEN

When I wake up, the message light is flashing. "Meet me at the Stewart Theater this morning at ten." That's all Smith says. I find it hard to believe I slept through his call. I am sure Nikita would not have slept through his call.

I have never heard of the Stewart Theater, so I look in the phone book. There's only one listing. I write the address down on the wall, along with Smith's real name. If something happens to me, I hope someone will be able to figure it all out. I spend the rest of the morning scribbling on the graffiti wall. Every word is honest. There are no lies on this wall. With all my markers, I unburden my loneliness, my shame, even my love for M. Of course only I know what I really mean. I can read between the lines. The smell of the markers makes me a little high.

At nine, I prepare for my rendezvous with Smith.

I dress for it as if it were a date. We are going to the theater, after all. I decide on a little Chinese shirtdress I got out of a bin in Chinatown. It's bright red. Very Mao Tse-tung. I complete the ensemble with a pair of black Sketchers, foot comfort being my new priority. On a whim, I put a fake mole on my cheek, but quickly realize I can't do it right; it looks more like an unsightly growth. I wipe it off. This screws up my makeup, and I end up wiping it all off, smudging my mascara. I can't be late, so I leave the house with freakish raccoon eyes. On the steps, I pass Stockbroker Guy. He gives me a serious once-over. Perhaps this look is working for me.

I get to the Stewart and find it is a gay porn theater. It is also a shit hole. Inside, I expect to find the underbelly of society, but it's mostly white, middle-aged businessmen. We all have our secrets. I wish that this could remain one for me. The floor is very sticky. I don't think it's from soda. My mother would not be pleased if she knew that I was here. I'm worried this is a ruse. It would be just like Smith to dick me around again. Here I am thinking I have him right where I want him and then—

"Parker."

I turn and see Smith. I ease gingerly into the seat next to him. "Come here often?" I say, not sure how to play this.

"When you reach my age, you realize the stupidity and narrow-mindedness of modern sexual mores."

On the screen some buffed guy is giving it to another guy up the old shoot. It looks painful. But I'm intrigued by the fact that Smith enjoys watching this. It's his escape. It's his nonreality. He seems more human to me, and I find that I'm no longer afraid of him.

"I got your message, Parker."

He stares at the screen the entire time. Engrossed.

"I'm going to need the money."

"Yes, I understood that."

He still hasn't taken his eyes from the screen. I find myself asking, "Don't you worry that someone will say something?"

"Everyone has something to lose by being here. It makes for a certain degree of détente."

A new guy just entered the frame. My eyes immediately gravitate to the enormous trunk between his legs. An uncircumcised penis. I realize I've never actually seen one of those live. Or close to live, anyway. It looks unruly. Sloppy. Strange. I feel decidedly unworldly.

"So, Parker, you wanted to discuss money. Discuss."

I remember Lil's mantra: *Do Bad Things.* "Now they want more."

"How much more?"

"Thirty. . . three, I mean five, thousand."

"Thirty-five thousand? What kind of number is that?" Smith shakes his head. "They are utter idiots. Toxic Avengers *indeed*—"

"You know who they are?"

"Of course. They call themselves 'Eco-Rectifiers,' if you can believe that." He sighs. "Every time a pigeon gets a stomachache near one of my plants, they jump all over me."

"If you know who they are, why don't we just call the cops?"

"That would make my wife very unhappy."

"I think your wife would be very unhappy if she knew you were sitting in a dump watching gay porn."

He dismisses the notion with a mere wave of his hand. "She understands that."

An emotion inside me stirs. I recognize it as envy. Smith can tell his wife about his gay porn fetish. That's the type of honesty that creates true intimacy. I'm not sure I'd be able to admit something like that. I'd live with the secret and die, having only lived half a life.

"Parker, you will have your money."

"I need it for Thursday."

"Let me know where and when. You've won this one. Congratulations. And incidentally . . ." He pauses for the money shot. "What was Lil doing sleeping in my daughter's bedroom?"

A good question. I've been wondering the same. "I think she was mad at you because you said you were out of town when you really weren't. Lil doesn't like it when plans change."

"No. I don't think that's it at all. Your friend Lil craves drama. She creates it."

He gets up to go, never having looked at me. I move my legs to the side so he can pass. I'm not ready to leave just yet. I watch the movie, thinking about Lil. I'm stunned by the precision of Smith's observation. She *is* the only person I know who does not lose herself by living vicariously through others. *Her* reality is the *only* reality. She never watches TV. She does watch Elvis movies, but only to analyze them with respect to American pop culture. She creates her own drama. Kicking gifts down the steps, crawling across strange terraces. Stealing plasma-screen televisions. Maybe this is really her show. Maybe I, Parker Grey, am merely a guest star.

Another money shot on-screen. There's a low murmur throughout the theater. Everyone is either masturbating themselves or someone else. My mother would stroke out. A bald head pops up in the seat in front of me. I thought the guy next to that seat was alone. Stupid me. I realize I recognize the head, although I can't quite place it. He feels me looking at him, because he turns and looks at me. Irritated, as if I'm breaking a cardinal rule of sorts, but then his expression changes. Because it's Vaughn.

"Sweetie?" He leans over the seat, discreet. "What are you *doing* here?"

I lean forward. "I'm blackmailing someone."

He just laughs his ass off. "You *are* fabulous! First Bonnie Cashin and now this!"

I get up to go. "I'd kiss you but . . ."

He raises his hand. "Understood."

He's the first person I haven't lied to in a long time. It feels refreshing and strangely safe.

TWENTY

Everything's back on track, and I decide to walk home, basking in the glory of what has turned out to be a perfect hair day. It's as if my tresses are a barometer of the larger picture as a whole. And judging from their splendor, things could not be better. In a few short days Lil will be free. I will be out of credit-card debt. I will finally be able to tell Lil about M. This may be my show, or it may be Lil's, but either way, it's number one in its time slot.

I should have known it was too good to be true.

As soon as I walk in the door, the phone rings. I grab it. It's Lil. She's babbling away, like a complete loon. I can't get a word in edgewise.

"He's the most *amazing* man I've ever met! I'm in *love*! I can't give you names so don't ask me. But I *love* him, Parker!"

"Lil! It's all going to be okay. I'm going to get you out of there. I'll have the money on Thursday—"

"He's *killing the birds,* Parker. He's such a bastard! *My own father.* I'm ashamed to be related to him. But it's not a surprise! He doesn't care about me. Why should he care about the yellow-shafted flicker? Fucker."

"Lil—" But she's not listening. She's too mired in her own drama.

"Parker, get us the money."

"What do you mean 'us'?"

"I mean I'm going with them. We can live off the money for a while."

The words send a chill through my spine. Lil has Stockholm syndrome. "Lil, you're coming home with me."

"No, I'm staying with them! They need me because I know the plants!"

"*What* plants?" I don't like the sound of this at all.

"We have to show him he can't *fuck* with the *fowl. Shipherd* says that's how it has to be, and *Shipherd* knows. *Shipherd's* the most amazing man I've ever met. . . ." And she's off babbling again. Lil can't possibly be in love with a guy named Shipherd. Unthinkable. She's talking so fast I have the urge to slap her.

"I have to go, Parker. We're doing it!"

"Doing *what*?"

"I'm with them. We're going to teach my fucking father and his *factories* a lesson or two. . . ."

She's going to pull a Patty Hearst on me. How much more of this can I take? She hangs up. I sit on the island, my head in my hands. Trying desperately to gather my wits. The phone rings again. I can barely muster the strength to answer it, but I do.

It's Caroline.

"I just talked to Vaughn." There's a silence. "I want in, Parker. I hate my life, and I want in."

I consider it. If I can get enough dirt on these Toxic Avengers, maybe I can somehow thwart what I'm certain is a half-brained scheme to blow up a factory. I could give the information to Smith. His people would handle it. Then Lil wouldn't get into any real trouble. At least not any serious trouble. I am Parker Grey. This is my show, that's clear now. I am the hero. Don't heroes always have a crack team? I've already got Trudy on board, sort of, as my spiritual guide. I decide to bring Caroline into the fold. "We have to work on a need-to-know basis."

"Absolutely."

"Okay, I need you to do some research. Find out everything and anything you can about a group that goes by the name Toxic Avengers." I tell her Smith's real name. "I want to know if there's any connection between him and this group. Find out all the plants that he owns, and see if you can figure out which one would be a prime target. It has to do with birds."

"Birds?"

"Yes." I try to remember the name of the bird Lil said. "The yellow-shafted flicker."

"Are you making this up?"

"No. I'm not sure that's exactly it, but it's got a name like that. Try to put together a . . . ." I can't think of the word.

"A profile."

"Yes, exactly. A profile."

"What's the time frame?"

"I'll need it fast. Really fast."

"When?"

"Wednesday."

"It'll be done. I'll be in touch."

The line goes dead. Caroline is Nikita, making the world safe for all us mere mortals.

★

I go outside for air and to pick up some Bufferin. My jaw is killing me, and we're all out. I walk to the Korean grocery and pay premium for a midget bottle. I also grab an ice cream bar. I haven't eaten all day. Walking home, it occurs to me that M may not be circumcised. I wonder what he's doing at this exact moment. Maybe he's working on his movie? Maybe he's sitting at home eating a meal? I wonder if he has a girlfriend. I wonder if he's lonely. I wonder what it would be like to rest my head on his shoulder. I'm full of wonder, until I get home and find two guys standing outside my apartment.

I crouch down on the stairwell below. They're both young, sort of doughy, as if they drink too much. One has brown hair, the other blond, otherwise the experience is similar. The one with the brown hair pounds his fist on my door. I don't understand why they don't ring the bell. It's not broken.

"What the fuck, Chief? She's not here."

"Chief . . . we've got no choice."

They both call one another Chief. What does this mean?

My heart starts to pound. Maybe they work for Smith? Maybe Smith was just screwing with me, and now he's sent these two to beat the hell out of me. Or worse. After all, I know about his gay porn fetish.

"Chief, we don't do this, we're gonna hear it. He's gonna kill us."

"Why the fuck can't he do it himself?"

"I heard ya, Chief, but orders are orders, and we're paid to follow orders. . . ."

I duck down and run out of the building. And I keep running. And I remember Tommy at work, saying that if I ever needed anything, I should come to see him.

★

"Parker? What the fuck are you doing here?" Tommy looks up from counting money. From the expression on my face, he knows something's wrong.

"There's these two guys." I'm out of breath. "Outside my door . . ." I'm also genuinely afraid and pissed at myself for believing my brilliant plan went off without a hitch. Smith was so calm, so cool. He didn't become a captain of industry because he's a warm, loving individual. He became a captain of industry because he's a ruthless prick! I wouldn't put it past him to try and have me knocked off. I blackmailed a man who is used to steamrolling people to get his own way! And now it's payback time. What is it the Chinese say? You eat, you pay. "They were pounding on my door. Creepy looking guys—"

"Sit down. Have a drink."

And for once I do. Tommy calls Vinnie and Joe, they're at the back table playing cards. They work as bouncers, but they spend most of their time offering the waitresses back rubs. Then they try to cop feels. Vinnie is obese and yet just about every waitress in the place has allowed him to perform oral on her. They say he's so physically repulsive, it makes one feel like a supermodel. Esme swears it did wonders for her self-esteem. Next to Vinnie, her slightly untoned body was sheer perfection. Self-esteem issues aside, I've never had the need to feel like a supermodel. And so I've refrained.

"I need you to go to Parker's place. Give 'em your keys, kiddo."

I hand them over gladly. Earlier in the year, a store owner on Greenwich was stalking one of the waitresses. She turned to Tommy for help, and he sent Vinnie and Joe to do the job. They threw a two thousand–pound mako shark through his window with a note on it that read, "You're next." The guy left her alone after that.

Vinnie and Joe leave, and I make myself comfortable in the back room. Laurel and Margaret are counting their money and having a couple smokes because they're too beat to walk home.

"Parker? What the fuck are you doing here?"

"Some guys were at my door. I got freaked out."

"Fuck . . . You sure it wasn't Doc?"

I shake my head no. I'm sure.

"Fucking loser crank called me last night, told my room-mate that he was a plumber and that he had to come over first thing in the morning to fix a pipe. I call my super, he doesn't know what the hell I'm talking about, so I'm sitting up at five A.M. with a fucking crowbar thinking some asshole is coming to rob me."

"Doc's a big joker."

"Girls! You're just in time."

I see Tommy wheeling in a brand-new karaoke machine. Laurel gets up to go. "Tommy. I'm not in the mood."

"Sit your ass down, I've been practicing all week." He plugs the thing in. I watch him as he messes with the settings. He reminds me of Ralph Kramden. He's so excited about it, it's almost endearing. Almost.

"You like to sing, Tom?"

"Love it."

Margaret looks at me. "Don't encourage him."

He pushes a button, and an old Bobby Darin song starts to play. Tommy bops along, tossing the mike back and forth in his hands. That's his move. The mike toss. Inspired. "She wore artificial flowers . . . artificial flowers . . ." He's channeling the spirit of Bobby Darin himself, a couple beads of sweat forming on his upper lip. But he's putting his all into it. And I realize, Tommy's a guy with a dream. All he ever wanted to do was sing, but instead he got stuck running a bar. Just like his father. The one who's spent time upstate. Behind our masks, we're all just people with dreams. Smith and his gay porn, Tommy and his karaoke, me and M.

"Tommy! You suck!"

He gives Laurel the finger and keeps on singing. And when the song ends, we all applaud like dutiful employees.

"Who's next?"

No one's taking.

"Someone's gonna sing a fucking song."

We all look away and then down.

"Parker. Get your ass up here and sing."

Since he's saving my life, I figure it's the least I could do. I get up and scan the song chart. But Tommy picks for me.

"I love this fucking song."

An old Carly Simon song, from back when James Taylor had hair. The words come crawling across the screen. Tommy's by my side, pointing to the words on the monitor, lest I don't understand the full concept of karaoke.

"You walked into the party . . . Like you were walking onto a yacht . . ."

My mind makes a jump. The lights of a carnival, it's night, I'm out with my friends. I'm ten. I own the world. And a boy named Alan wants to ride the Ferris wheel with me. Alan. The cutest boy in school. Our bare arms touching as we climb into the air. The Ferris wheel seems huge, and everything beneath us small, insignificant. And somewhere, this song is playing. Alan jokes that a song about veins is stupid. I laugh. It's not about veins, it's about *being vain*. Alan has no clue. Which only makes me adore him more. He could've picked ten other girls, but he picked me. The Ferris wheel, night. I'm ten. I've never been happier. Tommy has stopped pointing, the girls are all staring. And I'm having too much fun to care. My voice isn't what it once was, timid, pinched, thin. No, there's nothing timid about it anymore. I realize that I like to sing. When I finish, I hand the mike back to Tommy.

"Jesus Christ, Parker."

Laurel is impressed. "You've got a gift."

I shrug it off. I can carry a tune. At the very least, after a life spent with music, I should be able to do this.

"Your voice is amazing." Margaret doesn't think anything is amazing. Now I'm embarrassed. Tommy looks flustered. "What I wouldn't give to have an inch of what you have. And you're throwing it all away on law school?"

Laurel agrees. "It's such a waste, Parker."

It does seem like a waste. I make a mental note to tell them I quit law school. Tommy's adamant. "It's a gift."

"You think?"

They have no idea that I've been doing music my whole life. And yet because of that, or perhaps in spite of it, I'm completely humbled by their opinions.

"Who's next?"

And the night passes us by.

We take turns singing and laughing and telling stories. I feel so close to everyone. Tommy even makes us steak and eggs. Then he serenades us with Bobby Darin and stories about how he wanted to be a singer. I feel a sense of community. A sense of family. I don't want it to end. All of us here like this, being together and laughing and taking time.

"I knew this guy growing up, he could suck his own dick. He was incredibly limber. Could suck his own dick." Tommy's prattling on. "He's a TV actor, he's done a bunch of stuff. Of course he wouldn't know me from Adam, but it's a funny thing, 'cause every time I see him on a show, all I can think about is how we used to go to his house and watch him suck his own cock."

I think of M and am afraid. But then I remember that M is from Croatia. There's no way he ever knew Tommy back in Rockaway.

"That's pretty gay, Tom."

"It's not gay, Laurel. Yeah, I watched, but who wouldn't? We were totally envious of him. It was like a freak show or a train wreck. You can't turn away."

"Did you go over to his house a lot?"

"Maybe once a month. It was like the show of shows. . . . Who needed Ed Sullivan when we had Ritchie, the kid who could suck his dick?" Tommy cracks up.

"Frequency, Tom . . . that's troubling."

"What the hell are you talking about? We were kids. We didn't even know what a queer was."

"When I was young, I had an uncle who was gay. He was beaten to death by sailors who thought that he had stolen some codfish from them." Margaret really knows how to bring the conversation to a halt. She's like some modern-day Garbo. Very dry, very cool, very touch my monkey. "He died in the street, like an animal. Men in Iceland don't like gay people; they consider it an affront to their manhood. They would sooner cut off their dicks then have them touched by another man."

Tommy cracks up. "Iceland!" His rattling, alcoholic laugh

ends with him hocking up vast amounts of phlegm. "Where the cod are afraid!!"

It makes no sense, but none of this makes any sense. We're rapidly approaching the point where too much of a good thing becomes just that. It's almost five-thirty in the morning, and from the window I can see that the sky is beginning to brighten. We've pushed it too far. If we don't get out of here soon, someone's going to embarrass themselves. Everyone's pasty and worn. The eggs sit in my stomach like a brick. I'm pale and tired. I feel weak and sick all at the same time.

I turn and see Vinnie and Joe come in, manic energy surrounding them. There's a crazed look in their eyes, like they've been eating their young. I wonder if I'm going to find myself embroiled in a manslaughter case.

"Where have you been?" Tommy yells.

"We went down to Hogs and Heifers."

"What about Parker's guys?"

"Took care of them. Cocksuckers really gave us a hard time."

Joe comes over and starts rubbing my neck.

"Gave us the funniest excuse I've ever heard. Said they were scouts."

Tommy laughs. "Scouts? Like boy scouts?"

Even I'm confused. "Book scouts?"

"Who the fuck knows? We kicked the shit out of them. They won't be back anytime soon."

I'm grateful. "Thanks, you guys. . . ."

Joe slips his big, meaty hand under my shirt. I knew he

would do this. In his mind, it's payment. He wants a feel. I could move my arm forward to block his hand, but I don't. Tonight, I give it to him. He grazes the side of my breast and then moves up to my shoulders. He stays there, rubbing my shoulders, my neck, the top of my arms. It's been so long since I've been touched. I'll take it where I can. I feel my eyes closing in surrender.

TWENTY-ONE

It's nearly six-thirty in the morning when I get home, and I am eager to get inside before the light of day turns me to ash. I pass Stockbroker Guy on his way to work. He lets me in as I fumble for my keys. "Late night?"

He's going for friendly, but it comes off smarmy. I smile a tight, my-jaw-is-aching smile, but then a thought occurs to me. "Hey," I ask, "did anybody come knocking on your door last night? Around eleven or so?"

He shakes his head. "No . . . nobody. But there was a fight or something in the hall. Someone was trying to get into an apartment. You should watch out. Last week some assholes came in and stole my plasma screen. I came home from work, and it was gone. And I had my alarm on and every-thing."

No you didn't. I want to say that, but I don't. I'm a little surprised, actually. Even Stockbroker Guy is reinventing history, because he's too embarrassed to admit he was passed out, farting with his fly open, and didn't hear a thing as two girls yanked his screen off the wall.

"Like I said. Be careful."

"Thanks."

He gets into the black town car that pulls up for him and I climb the steps. My jaw continues to throb and I'm winded. I've got to lay off bad food. I'm going to start running every day. I'm going to go to the farmers' market and buy apples and goat cheese. I'm going to take better care of myself. I'm going to quit smoking. . . . I reach the top of the steps and see a note taped to the door. I pull if off and open it, half expecting a death threat from Smith.

We would like to use your apartment
for a movie we are shooting called True North.
Please contact us at the office. 212-555–8989

True North, the words bang around my brain like a pinball. *Where do I know that? Why does this sound familiar?* And then the camera pans in tight, real tight. It hovers on my stunned, poleaxed expression as it hits me: *True North* is the movie M is doing!

I can't get inside to the phone fast enough. M is doing a movie, and they want to use *my* apartment! It's kismet. It's fate. It's the greatest *fucking luck* I've ever had in my life! I call the number on the paper. It's not even seven in the morning.

I'll leave a message. Calm down, breathe. And then someone answers.

"Production?"

"Hi, I uh, got a note about you guys using my apartment—"

"Please hold."

I wait for what seems to be an eternity, and then a woman named Kim gets on the phone.

"Hi, what's your address?"

"Four eighty-five North Moore Street—"

"Right! Yeah, we want to use your apartment for a shoot this Friday. Typically, we pay four hundred a day. I know it's short notice, so we'll make it five hundred."

My heard is pounding. "Whatever, that's fine. What's the scene?"

"It's a dream sequence. Something about the lead guy learns that the woman he loved was lying to him. He figures it out in the dream. Something like that."

"So M will be in the scene?"

"Yeah, totally. I can probably get you an autograph if you like."

This offends me. I don't want an autograph. I'm not some stupid fan. "That's okay. I don't want any autographs."

"Okay . . . So, I'm just checking . . . . You have a big mural on your wall?"

"Mural?" I look at the Colorform wall. Is it a mural? A mural implies artistic intent. I was just covering a wall with colored paper. What to say? "Uhhh . . ." Pick an answer. "Yes. Yes I do."

"Oh yeah, I've got your file. I couldn't find it . . ."

They have a file. How do they have a file? Is Smith behind this?

"Yeah, they're interested in your walls. The mural and the one with all the words."

The Bonnie Cashin graffiti wall.

"So don't go painting them or changing anything."

My head is spinning. *How does she know this?*

"Figure that we'll get there around four o'clock for the prelight."

Prelight. "Okay. And I can be here?"

"Of course. It's your apartment. We'll see you Friday. Oh, and just so you know. You should be really careful in your building. Two of our location scouts got the shit knocked out of them last night."

My mouth goes dry. I ordered the hit. "Are they okay?"

"Yeah, a couple broken ribs and a broken nose, but other than that they're okay. We'll see you Friday."

I hang up, riddled with guilt. Those poor guys. But my guilt is overshadowed by the sheer joy of knowing that M is coming to my apartment on Friday. We will meet here! And I will cling to the first thing that makes sense.

Until then, I must stay in character.

Parker Grey must save her best friend. She must bring down the Eco-Rectifiers. She must pay off her credit-card debt. She must buy a snazzy new outfit. And then, and only then, can she meet the man of her dreams.

Friday. Just a few short days. I must stay focused.

★

I have a sneaking suspicion that the Eco-Rectifiers may be dumb enough to still have Colin Richards's cell phone. I phone the number and key in a text message. My suspicions are confirmed when they phone me back promptly. Such amateurs.

They put Lil on the phone. I hold my breath, uncertain what to expect.

"How're you holding up?"

"*Shipherd's* opened my eyes to a lot of things, Parker. I don't think I'm ever going to be the same. I really *love* him. . . ."

I know that Lil could never love a guy named Shipherd like I know that the sky is blue. It's just not in her. She could never love a man who wore bad shoes; she could never love a man who had a mustache. She could never love a guy named Shipherd. Period. This crazy babble has to be a lack of protein.

"I spoke to Smith, Lil. He's getting me the money. We can do this Thursday night, just like Shipherd said."

"That'll work because *Friday* we're going after the fucker! Come with us, Parker. I told him how much you *love* birds. . . ."

I detest birds. I was attacked by a bird as a child. I've never gotten over it. Lil knows this. Either she's insane, or she's screwing around. But why would she screw around? She begins to spout about the yellow-shafted flicker, also known as *Colaptes auratus*. Rattling off a litany of obscure facts. How she remembers so much, so fast, is a testament to her immense intelligence. And the fact that she's never really put it to good use. "Lil . . . Let me talk to Shipherd."

She puts him on the phone.

"I'll have the money for you Thursday. I want you to let her go."

"She's a big girl. She's not going to be pushed around any-more by her father or you or any other patriarchal bastard bent on breaking her down and forcing her to sell her soul."

Sell her soul? Whatever has given him this impression? Lil has never worked a day in her life. She just studies. With the ardor of a Talmudic scholar. I always tell her that in another life she was a rabbi, and she never argues with me. "So you *don't* want the money?

"Of *course* I want the money. And if you don't bring it, she's ready to die for the cause."

"And which cause is this?"

"The fucking yellow-shafted flickers!!! Her father is mas-sacring them! *Stop fucking around, Parker!*"

"I'm getting the money Thursday. When do you want to meet?"

"Midnight at Pier Forty-seven."

"Pier Forty-seven?" This is not *Starsky and Hutch*. There will be no midnight chases on piers. There will be no deserted warehouses, either. I am not a cliché. "How about we just do it someplace more public? Like Grand Central?"

"No!"

I hear mumbling in the background. Lil's bitching at him. This is a good sign. One week in, and she's already giving him a hard time.

"Fine. The Port of Authority."

I can't tell if he's speaking metaphorically, or if he's just a moron. "Port of Authority it is."

"The new building. New Jersey Transit. Meet inside Gate 108. And make it eleven-thirty."

"Okay. Eleven-*thirty*. I'll be there."

"And no funny stuff! Or we'll kill her."

"Don't worry." I hang up from nonreality. I have an appointment with Caroline.

Stay focused.

TWENTY-TWO

Caroline and I meet over burgers at the Corner Bistro. After my last conversation with Lil, I feel *I* need protein. Caroline is in a good mood. She's wearing these fabulous pointy glasses from Morgenthal Frederics that only she could pull off. She looks like a cross between Jackie O. and Catwoman.

"Making progress?"

"You wouldn't believe."

The waitress comes, we order, and then get down to business. Caroline pulls out an overwhelming stack of papers. "Don't worry, it's all been condensed. These are my notes." She waves a smaller sheaf of papers at me. "What you don't know about me, what no one knows about me, is that I went to J school at Columbia."

"You're kidding."

"Nope."

"I had no idea."

"I never talk about it. For a while there, it was just a play I was in."

I know what that's like.

"I had big plans, but they never happened, or I never bothered trying to make them happen. I blew it. Totally blew it . . ." Her voice trails off, as if she's too disgusted with herself to elaborate. She hands me a typewritten report. "So, here's what's going on. It's a first draft."

I scan the pages. "Tell me what you know."

"The Toxic Avengers are part of a larger group known as ELF—they're a reactionary environmental group. They're all about consumer sabotage."

"ELF as in elves?"

"Yeah, they refer to themselves as elves."

"How come I've never heard of them?"

"Because the legit environmental groups hate them. They disavow everything the ELFs stand for. The Toxic Avengers are a splinter group—they formed about two years ago. From what I can gather, they were booted out of ELF, but ELF still sanctions them because they do a lot of damage. They've spilled raw sewage into a small-town river and then blamed it on the local plant. They've stolen toxic waste and dumped it into a bunch of ponds outside Schenectady, then they tried to lay it on the local nuclear plant. They do shit and blame it on other people. But last year, word on the street is that they stuck a bomb in J. G. Wendeborn's car."

J. G. Wendeborn: aka Mr. Smith.

"So I dug into Wendeborn, as you suggested." She looks at me over her glasses. "Am I to understand that you're . . . familiar . . . with him?"

This is a loaded question. The hero must keep some secrets to herself. I nod my head slightly. "I have been . . . in touch . . . with Mr. Wendeborn."

A small smile creeps across her face. She leans forward. "Wendeborn grew up poor, your basic Horatio Alger story. His dad worked on an assembly line at an ink factory in New Rochelle, one of those guys who saved every dime he ever made. He died with a couple hundred grand in the bank, but in sixty years he never bought himself a new winter coat. So the father dies, and J. G., the only son, gets all this money, and he goes out and buys the ink factory."

"Sort of poetic."

She nods. "It is. So now he's in the ink business. And he's good at it. He turns a profit at the factory, and then he buys another one in Rockaway. He made a small fortune running them."

"Ink. Who knew?"

"So of course, from there he got into real estate and corporate mergers, blah blah blah, and now he's one of the richest men in the world and all that, but he always kept the ink factories."

"Nostalgia?"

"Something. Maybe he wants to stay connected, so he doesn't forget where he came from. I don't know. But he still has both of them. And what's interesting is that the one in Rockaway is next door to a bird sanctuary—"

"You're joking."

She shakes her head. She's not. "It's been rumored that he's not meeting antipollution standards, and guess who gets sick from that?"

"The yellow-shafted flickers?"

She nods her head. "The yellow-shafted flickers."

Who knew a bird could promote such intrigue?

She shows me photos of the factory, belching out toxic levels of ink fumes, or whatever the hell it is. "My guess is that if the Toxic Avengers are looking to get to—"

"Smith."

She looks at me. Nods her head slowly, getting it. "*Smith*. They're going to be looking at taking out the target in Rockaway."

"How difficult would it be?"

"Not hard at all. He's got maybe forty workers working eight-hour shifts, and then there are only a few guys working the night shift. The security guard is learning Italian. He's more worried about irregular verbs than trespassers."

"Do you have any names?"

"Not yet. But I did some research, and a lot of the people in ELF went to Wesleyan."

"Tell me they're angry rich kids, and I'll vomit."

"I'm not sure. But if they went to Wesleyan, then they had a club, and if they had a club, I'll get names. . . . I know a guy who went there, he's very tapped into the alumni thing, so I'll see what I can find."

I think of Shipherd. He's the ringleader. "Look for a guy named Shipherd. I don't have a last name on him."

"How many guys named *Shipherd* can there be? I'll see what I can find out."

"But you'll be done by tomorrow?"

"Totally. Actually, I want to talk to you about this. I don't know what you're planning, but I have a friend, an old friend, actually a former boyfriend, who works over at Reuters. He's always been nagging me to get back into it and . . ." She cringes. "I told him about this."

I hold my breath.

"Don't freak out. It was all on the q.t. Reporters can be really discreet when they have to be. Anyway, he wants to run this as an article."

My heart pounds. My face heats up. This could actually work. "Are you serious?"

"Yeah, he says he can sell it."

"When would they run it?"

"All I need to do is confirm a few sources and punch it up a bit—"

"It has to be on *Friday. Friday early edition*. It can't be Thursday! Thursday will ruin everything!"

Caroline looks at me calmly.

"Otherwise I'm fucked." Actually, Lil's fucked. I'm fucked by proxy. *Focus. Breathe.*

"You're trying to avert something, aren't you?"

"I am, but I don't want to say anything more."

"You don't have to."

"Friday."

She nods. "Friday."

TWENTY-THREE

I unburden myself on the Bonnie Cashin graffiti wall, trying to quiet all the words inside my head. On the plasma screen, *Romeo and Juliet*. No volume, just pure cinema. Just South Beach on acid and the angst of young, perfect love. And the words pour out of my brain, through the markers, and onto the walls. But my hair is everywhere, driving me crazy. I pull a red elastic band off my wrist and over my hair. It snaps off and falls to the ground. I bend to pick it up. A red elastic band.

And I remember the first time I saw Dana.

I was reaching down to pick up an elastic band. It had fallen from my wrist, just like now. I bent down, in the lobby of Juilliard, and I saw him. He turned a corner and appeared. He was wearing a tux. He had a performance. I remember in that instant thinking he looked amazing in the tux. I followed behind him. I had to meet him.

Why? I don't know.

I followed him into Alice Tully Hall. I stayed for the entire performance. He was first chair. He was young, very young to be first chair. I was impressed. He commanded respect; his playing was precise, technically perfect, focused. It all came so easily for him. He made it seem so simple, so effortless. Fluid. After the performance, I slipped a note into his case and left.

He called the next week.

A month later we were living together, and day after day, I became smaller and smaller, until one day I looked into a mirror and I was gone. And his pills. His moods. Me trying to save him, him trying to do himself in, me blaming myself, him blaming me, me blaming me. The depression. His. Mine. Ours. The never-ending cycle of it all. If I'd just left the elastic band on the floor, I would've missed him. The mere act of putting my hair up altered the course of my life. Four years gone. Wasted; and everything that came before it, obliterated.

If I could just go back.

But I can't, so this time I leave the elastic band on the floor.

Romeo and Juliet are moving toward one another at the party. They've no idea what's in store for them. They move without intent. Toward their fate. And just like that, something goes off inside my head. And there it is. Music, inside my head. Clear. Sonorous. A song. I hum it to myself aloud, in solfège. *Sol, sol me, re, do re do, si* . . . Simple, spare, lyrical. I wonder where I've heard it, but I can't remember. It bothers me. Why can't I remember this simple song?

Then I know.

I've never heard it before.

It's my own song. All mine. Just like that.

I remember Dana again, that very first day I watched him play onstage. His playing, so simple, so effortless. I watched him because it was never easy for me. It was always a struggle. A good struggle, but a struggle nonetheless. And there he was, and he made it all seem the way it should be. I think, maybe I know now why I followed him. Maybe I never wanted him. Maybe I just wanted to be *like* him. Like what I thought he was. I wanted his ease. And now here it is. My song. Just like that.

Reaching down for an elastic band.

The first time I turned the wrong way.

This time, I've found the right way.

And Romeo's looking at Juliet through the big glass fish tank. It's all so simple. So perfectly simple.

TWENTY-FOUR

One more shift. One more day. The countdown begins. I head into the bar, and pass Tommy on his way out. He pats me on the back and turns to one of the regulars, "This girl has *some fucking* voice. Like *nothing* you've ever heard. I'm gonna get her to quit law school and go into the music business."

Little does he know.

I head inside, and I'm a minor celebrity. Tommy's been telling everyone about our karaoke powwow. I didn't think it was *that* big a deal. I duck in the back to marry bottles of ketchup. The girls from the last shift are heading out. Laurel and Esme are working tonight. Alden's outside. If I time it correctly, I could get a good back rub. Esme accosts me with a quick hug. I really like her. Even though she tried to come between M and me, she's got a good heart.

"Parker, you've *got* to sing for me! I can't believe I missed it. I went to lunch with Laurel; it's all she talked about."

"Really?"

"Don't play modest, Parker. Don't think for a minute I didn't think you had something else going on in that life of yours."

"What's that mean?"

"You're so not ever going to be a lawyer. It's not in your aura, or whatever you want to call it."

"Maybe . . ."

"Lawyers are all assholes, and you're not an asshole. Therefore, you can't become a lawyer."

★

The shift starts, and we are slammed. Totally slammed on a Wednesday. Very odd. Slogging through the bar, delivering beer and burgers to people who barely acknowledge my existence, I think about how indicative this is of how I see myself in the world. I've always felt, to a certain degree, invisible. Try as I do to connect, I never really can. It's too uncomfortable. It's like we're all running on a current, but my circuitry is backward. I can't remember a time when I didn't feel this way. Even with Lil, the parameters of our friendship have always been decidedly loose. We share, but we don't share. We open up, but we remain closed.

For a moment, I'm overwhelmed by all that separates me from everyone else. Then that old Sly and the Family Stone song comes on. The bartender turns up the volume, and I see a change come over everybody, from the waitresses to the customers. I drop off a couple beers to two guys at a table, and they're singing along. Hell, we're all singing along. And for once I don't see it as a bunch of stupid people, acting like fools. I see it as a statement of shared humanity. Everyone's here, now. And for this moment, we're all connected by the melody. In the moment with the song.

And I remember why I played music.

I played because it was the only way for me to feel connected.

The song ends and the customers return to their conversations, and I go back to being invisible. But it's okay because for me the memory remains.

And I wonder, how did I ever get so far off track?

★

Ten P.M. I've scheduled a quick convo with Caroline. Then I will call Smith. Due to the FBI phone tap situation, I'm not about to call him from the tavern. "Esme . . . Cover for me? I want to run to Googies."

"No problem sweetie . . . Get some almond cookies."

I hop over the fence that separates the outdoor seating area from the sidewalk and head down to Googies. Their almond cookies are a big favorite at the bar.

Caroline is waiting for me outside. She looks like hell.

"I need a smoke. I've been at this since yesterday—haven't even had time to sleep." She grabs a smoke out of my pocket as we duck into the doorway of the building next door. It's all very furtive. "You ready for this? That guy Shipherd . . . his father is the former head of *Firestone* tires."

"No shit." This is exactly what I said would make me vomit. We're not even dealing with a professional. We're dealing with a spoiled rich kid with an overactive sense of entitlement. Which, now that I consider it, might make him more dangerous than I thought.

"He's been booted out of every school from Choate to Wesleyan. He's accomplished nothing in life except for a long line of rap sheets that were swept under the carpet because his father isn't afraid to write checks. Anyway, he joined ELF right before he got expelled from Wesleyan."

"What'd he get expelled for?"

"He took a shit on a chemistry teacher's car."

"Class act."

"That was two years ago. You're dealing with a loose cannon. My sources say he's very emotional. Highs and lows."

"Bipolar?"

"I don't know. But ELF kicked him out, and that's when he started the Toxic Avengers. He recruited a couple disgruntled freshman flunkies. He even had outfits designed."

"Outfits."

"Yeah, you know, costumes."

"Like superheroes."

"Yeah."

"What a loser."

"Yes, he is. But in the last two years, he's been investigated twice for buying bulk shipments of *fertilizer*."

We both know what this means.

"His dad has gotten him out of trouble both times. That's the bad news. The good news is that the FBI has a file on him.

He does anything wrong, red flags go up. So, when the article rolls—"

"Flags will be raised!" This couldn't be more perfect! I will tip off the FBI with the pay phone at the bar, and then we'll drive the nail into the coffin with the article. My ratings are soaring! "What about Smith and the birds? Is he really killing them?"

"Yes and no. His plant isn't the greatest thing for the environment, but it's nothing compared to the pollution from Kennedy Airport. Not to mention the wastewater treatment plants that dump two hundred and fifty million gallons a day into Jamaica Bay. So could he do better? Yes. But is he deliberately hurting birds? No. Besides, his wife's on the board of the Audubon Society."

Smith's a mogul with issues, but he's no bird killer.

She smiles. Hands me her pièce de résistance.

"And they're running it?"

She nods.

I try to stay in character, cool and calm, but the real me seeps out of the edges. I have to hug her. It's all so exciting. It's just like on TV. Life imitating art, imitating life.

"We *kicked ass,* Parker. I couldn't have done this without you. And it just keeps getting better. AP needs a staff writer in their Athens offices—"

"Athens, *Greece*?"

She's giddy. "I quit my job, and I'm going."

"What?!"

"It was something that was offered to me out of J school. I turned it down, but the offer still stood, and now I'm thinking what the hell—"

"You're actually *going*?"

"I leave tomorrow morning. I can't believe it. It's a standing offer; it's been there for a while. I just wasn't ready. Now I am."

I feel sad. We were just becoming friends, really, and now she's going to leave.

"I know it seems crazy, but nothing ever seems to make sense, and then all this happened, and finally—"

I finish her sentence for her. "Something made sense, and so you're clinging to it."

"Exactly. And Athens is just the start. We can keep in touch by E-mail. And you can get your ass on a plane and come visit me."

I see us meeting in Paris for coffee. Or maybe in Italy, for a fashion show. My friend Caroline, the world reporter. Suddenly, it's all very glamorous.

"Before I forget, Vaughn wants you to call him. He wants you to play at his boyfriend's club." She writes his number down on the back of a matchbox and hands it to me. "Call him. Promise me."

And I do. I promise that I will call him, but I don't say when. I'm happy for her. As if my faith in the system has somehow been restored. Maybe it was bound to happen. It's not like we were going to spend the rest of our lives depressed, meeting in some bodega over eggs with cheese. Although most mornings it seemed like it was. We hug. "As soon as you get there, I want a phone call. Numbers, E-mails, all of it."

"I promise. I'll be seeing you again soon, Parker. I've got a good feeling about all this."

And I have a feeling that I'll be friends with Caroline for the rest of my life. As she heads off, I realize I've never lied to her. I've always just been myself and for her, that's enough.

★

I buy a dozen almond cookies in Googies and get change for the pay phone in the corner. Why is Smith covering for Shipherd? Maybe he's friends with his father. Maybe they do business together. Maybe it's all too mortifyingly embarrassing. The ruling class never likes to air dirty laundry. Who knows anymore? Life is very strange, and people are stranger. I make my call. Smith answers on the first ring.

"Hello, Parker."

"How'd you know it was me?"

"You're the only person with this number. Get to the point."

"They want the money tomorrow."

"Where would you like it?"

"I want you to bring it to the storage lockers at the Marriott hotel. Leave the key with the concierge under the name Trudy Sarandopolis. She's an employee at the bar. Have them deliver the key to her personally."

"And then we will be done."

"I suppose so."

"I think you will go far in life, Parker."

"Thanks." I'm strangely pleased that he thinks so. He is, after all, a captain of industry.

"After tomorrow we will consider this all done. And I mean everything. Please tell Lil I do not wish to see her again."

The ego on this guy. "I'll relay your sentiments."

"Thank you."

I sense a faint twinge of regret on my part as I hang up. Not really regret. Just the sensation that I'll never speak to this person again. Ever.

★

I get back to the bar and give Esme her cookies. All the tables have turned, and all hell's breaking loose. Everyone wants beer, everyone wants a check, some girl with gobs of makeup is complaining because her salad has too much dressing. But I don't care. It's just beer and salad dressing. It's nothing to get all crazy about. I've been hanging out with captains of industry in gay porn theaters. I'm going to tip off the FBI, and according to all the girls I work with, I'm going to be the next best thing. And for once, none of it is a lie.

★

We get through the night. Somehow. And now Esme and I sit in the back, totaling up our tips. It was a good shift. "I made nearly two hundred dollars."

Esme looks surprised. "Were you blowing the customers?"

I have no idea how I did it because frankly, my service really sucked. "Take twenty."

"What for?"

"You covered my tables, just take it."

"No, I'm not taking it. Sometimes we have great nights; just enjoy it. Treat yourself to something."

"Esme, take it." She knows she won't win the argument. She takes the twenty. Irked. I take a sip of her beer.

"Do you know that when I was fifteen my mother shipped me off to this drug rehabilitation program?"

Esme sometimes becomes reflective after her shift. She usually tells me some little tidbit that's out of left field, completely unrelated to anything we've discussed the entire night. "Really?"

"She just shipped me off because she thought I was on drugs. But I wasn't. I was just depressed. I lived there for a year. It was fucking horrible. I'm thinking of writing about it."

"A memoir?"

"Yeah, I want to call it *Esme on Esme*."

"You should do that."

"I think I will. Thanks for listening, Parker. I value your opinion."

I think that over time, I've come to know a lot more about Esme than I realized. I know that she quit school. I know that she has had an abortion. I know that she likes lilacs.

"I'll see you later. I'm gonna splurge on a cab tonight." She pulls on a sweatshirt. "Hey, whatever happened to that actor guy?"

"Who?"

"That hot guy who came in here. The one who's on that show. You know, he came in, he's doing a movie. I can't remember his name."

I'm not about to tell her he's coming over tomorrow. "Why do you ask me?"

"He came in a couple of times when you weren't working. He asked about you."

"He did?" I can feel my face burning up.

"Yeah."

"What'd he ask?"

"I don't know. Vague shit. Nothing in particular, just if you were going to be working or if I knew when you were working."

"Are you serious?"

"Yeah."

"How come you never told me?"

"I don't know. Guess I forgot."

"Esme!" My mask hits the floor and smashes into a thousand pieces.

"Sweetie . . . You *like* this guy?"

"No, it's not that." But it is that. I'm ready to bounce off the walls. A million questions running through my brain at once. "What did he say? Exactly! Tell me *exactly*!" I'm practically out of breath.

"Look at you! *'Exactly.'* Parker?!? This is so not like you! You're so even keeled and icy cool! Guys always say you're—"

"Who talks about me? Who notices me?" *I'm supposed to be invisible. What the fuck is going on?*

"Guys, lots of them. All the bartenders. They're afraid of you."

"Afraid?"

"Not afraid, intimidated."

"But why?'

"Because you're intimidating."

"How so?"

"You just are. You have a presence."

"Now I have presence?"

"Cut it out. You know it. All that hair, and the way you move, all like a cat."

"I move like a cat?"

"Not like a cat, you just have a way of moving. You move your hands in this way, I don't know. You do it all the time."

"Do what?!"

"You just have an air about you, a way about you that isn't like anyone else. And I mean that in the best possible way."

I am stunned. Completely stunned. All this time I thought people took me for some scrappy misfit. Then my mind returns to M.

"What did you say to M?"

"Who?"

"The guy! The actor guy!"

"I thought he was stalking you or something, so I always lied to him."

"You *lied*?!"

"Of course. Trust me, I've dated actors."

She shoves her money into her bra, takes one last drag of her smoke, and puts it out in the glass of warm beer. "I have to go. Jeez, you're all in a tizzy. Have a drink and relax."

I stare at it, as the water seeps up the paper and puts it out. M has been coming into the bar asking about me. The bartenders think I'm intimidating. I move like a cat. All this time I thought this was just a show about a girl who saves her kidnapped friend. Apparently, I haven't been seeing the whole picture.

TWENTY-FIVE

Tomorrow has arrived, today is here, and I'm off to save Lil. En route on the B train to Times Square, I visualize everything.

I will see Trudy, she will give me the key to the locker, and I will get the money. I will place the money into my knapsack. I will leave the suitcase in the ladies' room. I will head to the dentist for my jaw splint. An officious attendant will spot the sleek silver briefcase in the bathroom. She will think it is a bomb. As would I, if I were she. They will lock the doors of the building before I am able to leave. I will be trapped. My prints will be on the case. The FBI will find me. Smith will tell them I was blackmailing him. I will be imprisoned. I will become a love slave to an evil warden, who bears a striking resemblance to Chuck Connors. This is my future. Or it's a TV movie I once saw.

Breathe through the anxiety and rewind.
Reenvision The Plan, with new writers.

I will meet Trudy, I will get the money, I will ditch the suitcase. I will go to the dentist. Then, I will buy a snazzy outfit. I will stash my thirty-five thousand at the bar, then I will go home and double condition my hair with the conditioner Lil brought from Japan that contains bovine—we hope—placenta. Two hours later, my hair will be perfection. After a light meal, I will go to the Port Authority to get situated. I know the place like the back of my hand. Years of riding the New Jersey Transit bus line back and forth from my mother's house to the city for lessons will finally pay off. I know the terminal, I know the schedules, I know the drivers.

But I'm forgetting something. I'm forgetting The Confession. Today I have decided I will confess to Trudy that I am a liar. It's going to be the most painful part of The Plan.

★

The lobby of the Marriott is packed. I wait ten minutes just to get an elevator. I remind myself to breathe. There is plenty of time. The elevator finally arrives, and when the doors open at the restaurant, I can see Trudy's saved us a small table by the window. She's already ordered two salads. "Hey kiddo! I believe this is for you." She hands me an envelope. I peek inside and see the locker key. She doesn't ask me anything. She has just done this for me. A random act of friendship. This is why I have to confess.

"I got you dressing on the side. They drown it here."

"Thanks." We sit down.

"This is so nice. So civilized. We should do this more often."

I nod my head. We should. I admire the view for a moment. It's almost as pretty as it is at night. Another waitress drops off our salads. I'm not all that hungry. I push an orange slice around the plate.

"So what's up? What have you been up to?"

"Not much." I'm already lying. I've promised myself I wouldn't lie. It's part of The Plan. I have to do this. I have a knot in my stomach, like I'm about to go on trial.

"You okay? You seem out of it."

I want to talk to her. I want to confess, and I'm avoiding it. I am a bad person. That's the feeling that floods over me. But I have to talk, I have to open up my mouth and speak. Or I'm going to be stuck in this place forever. "I've done some bad things." From the look on her face, it's the last thing she was expecting me to say.

"Jesus, what? Have you killed someone?"

"No! Not like that." I'm stuck again. Like the words are trapped in quicksand. They try to come out but get pulled back down. Two escape. "It's just . . ." It's just. I don't know where to begin. I push the words out of me. It's like giving birth. "Ever since I can remember, I've always wanted to be someone else. It's never been enough to be just me."

Trudy has her Dr. Drew Pinsky face on. "That's because your dad left when you were six."

"It's not that simple—"

"Yeah, of course it is. Your sense of self wasn't fully developed; you were at a point when you needed him. If he'd left when you were twelve, things would be different. You would've been pushing him away anyway. But at six. Well, at six, you got fucked."

But I know that really isn't it. "Trudy, I'm just such . . ." My voice is giving out on me. "A liar." I've said it. I've let it out. I keep going. "I make up things about myself that aren't true, and then I go to great lengths to make people think they are true. I did when I was young, and then I stopped for a while, but I started again. And now, it's to the point where I can't have certain people ever meet one another. Like, I told everyone at the bar I was in law school. I'd panic whenever you came by, after you broke up with John. I was terrified he'd tell you I was in law school. I lived in fear of it. I figured you'd find out, and you'd hate me."

She opens her mouth to speak, but I keep on talking, fast. "And it's *worse*. I lie about *everything*. I'm a musician, Trudy. I've studied music my whole life. It's what I do, it's the only thing I know how to do, and I quit and I couldn't admit that to anybody. And I lived with a guy who popped pills, which you know, but what you *don't* know is that I lost my mind. I lost everything. I wanted to walk in front of cars. I couldn't manage to get out of bed, and then when I finally left, I didn't know who the hell I was anymore. But I knew I was more than what I felt like, more than what I was reduced to. So I started lying again. I'm a *liar. A big, fat liar.*"

I've said it. I've told her what my mask is. I think I feel better, or maybe humiliation has replaced guilt. Maybe I feel worse. Is this what absolution is supposed to feel like?

"Lying is a good way to keep people at a distance. It's a good way to make sure no one gets close."

I can't look at her. I just stare at the orange on my plate.

"Kiddo. You gotta give yourself a break." Trudy isn't mad. "You think you're the only person who ever told a lie or two?"

I shrug, my body language that of a two-year-old.

"We *all* tell lies. People ask you how you're doing, you say, 'Great!' But you don't mean it . . . it's a lie. We weave in and out of truth because truth is very subjective."

"But I told all these people—people that I like—that I was in law school. . . ."

"Well, now you'll tell them that you dropped out. It wasn't for you. And you'll never mention it again."

I nod my head.

"You were lost, that's all."

"I've been lost my whole life."

"Maybe so, but why are you beating yourself up for it? It's not like it's a genetic flaw. You're here now, and this is the only life you have, so give yourself a break. Stop staring at the orange on your plate, and move on."

She's right. The choice is mine.

"Jeez, kiddo, did you really think I'd be that mad at you for saying you were in law school?"

I nod.

"You have to stop being so scared. Just be yourself."

"I don't know who that is."

"Then fake it until you do. Fake it, and eventually it'll seem real. Just pretend you're on a show."

I exhale. Maybe I'm not as lost as I thought. *"The Parker Grey Show."*

"*Exactly!* And I can make guest appearances."

"You already have." And for the final hurdle. "So you for-give me?"

"There's nothing to forgive. You're my friend. It's a for-eign concept, but you'll get used to it."

The weight of the world begins to lift off my shoulders. The dark cloud hovering overhead begins to dissipate.

"Eat. Before your leaves sog up."

And I do. I'm starving. It's been days since I've actually eaten. "M's coming over tomorrow night."

"*What?!*"

"They're using my apartment as a location for the movie he's in."

"And he's coming?"

"He is."

"Holy fucking shit, Parker. Do you know what that's called?"

"Kismet?"

She shakes her head. "It's destiny."

"I don't believe in destiny."

"Pessimist."

"I don't. I wish I did, but I only believe in chance. And I don't even know if you can believe in that. But it gets weirder. Remember how he was coming into the bar and I couldn't talk to him because I didn't want him to think of me as, I don't know, whatever it is that I'm not yet, or something?"

"Yeah."

"I found out yesterday that it turns out he was coming in when I wasn't working and asking Esme about *me*."

Trudy's on the verge of a conniption. *"Get out."*

"What do you think that means?"

"Well, I don't think it means he really likes the way you pour a beer!"

"And then they want to use my apartment for a location. What are the odds?"

"It's fucking destiny, Parker."

"It is not! It can't be. Destiny only happens to other people. Destiny doesn't happen to pathological liars—"

"You're not pathological. Did Esme tell him where you live?"

"I don't think so."

"Well, destiny or chance, this *is it,* kiddo!"

"I'm freaking out. I'm double conditioning my hair tonight with Japanese placenta and then—"

She cuts me off. "No! You can't. You can't do *anything* like that."

"Why not? My hair will look amazing."

"Your hair already looks amazing."

She looks as if she may bite me, so I don't argue.

"Do you double condition your hair any other night?"

"I do it every now and then." Which is a lie. "Actually, I've only done it once before."

"Then don't do it. Be yourself. You have to be yourself. You have to let it all hang out. Don't you see, Parker? If you want to be true to yourself, then you can't double condition your hair."

Who knew double conditioning could be such a bad thing?

"That's what you do wrong. You try to be someone else,

and then you end up distorting yourself. That's what happened with your last boyfriend. You were trying to be someone else. From the get-go, you were trying to be what you thought he wanted you to be, instead of just being who you are."

"And the double condition is really going to ruin everything?"

"It's symbolic, or metaphoric, or . . ." She's getting flustered. "Just promise me you won't do it. If you do, it'll be a *pox* on your entire relationship."

"Jesus, Trudy, a pox?"

"A *malocchio*." She makes the evil-eye hand signal. Then she narrows her gaze and gets all old-world Greek on me. "Promise me no double condition."

I promise.

"Promise me you won't do anything different. No gobs of makeup, no sultry lip gloss."

"Can I at least wear something that makes me look good?"

"Yeah, but don't buy anything new."

Cross the snazzy new outfit off the list.

"Anything that you would normally do is fine. You can cut your toenails, shave your pits, wear deodorant. But nothing else. You're going to just be you, you're going to lay yourself out there like a big dead fish."

"What if he throws me back in?"

"He throws you back in, you're not really dead. So you'll swim away, and you'll be fine."

She says it with such certainty. *I'll be fine. I am fine.*

"Talk to him. Go up to him and talk to him, and don't let

anything stop you. If he doesn't make the first move, then you do it. He's just a person, Parker. That's all. Flesh and blood. He's got a mother and a father. He takes a crap in the morning after coffee. He's just a person. Don't let the rest fool you."

★

Just a person my ass.

I'm back in the lobby, and I'm thinking that if I spit on the ground three times and put a bulb of garlic in the bathroom, I should be able to reverse Trudy's pox and still double condition. I understand her point, but I want my hair to look good. I hand my key to a perky concierge who disappears into a back room and emerges with one of those metal cases that Smith is so fond of. She tells me to have a great day. A big Marriott smile plastered to her face.

"Can you tell me where the ladies' room is?"

"Certainly, down the corridor to the left, pass the bank of phones, turn right, and then you'll see a door at the end of the corridor. Go through the door, turn right and then a quick left."

She lost me at *certainly*.

Ten minutes later, I finally find the bathroom. The attendant gets up from her chair as soon as she sees me. I feel bad for her because, let's face it, being a bathroom attendant really sucks. "Please don't get up on account of me." She nods, gives a funny wave of her hand. It's a combination of "Thanks" and "If you only knew." Then she sits back down, towel in hand, armed for the next intruder. I go into the far stall and put the metal case on the toilet. I almost don't want to open it. What if Smith's screwed me again? But he hasn't. It's all here.

I've never seen so much cash in my life.

I can only imagine what the attendant might think if she were to see it. I transfer it to my knapsack. I consider leaving the briefcase in the stall, but the Chuck Connors Alabama State Penitentiary scenario comes to mind, and I think better of it. On the way out I stick two hundred–dollar bills into her tip cup. She's busy offering deodorant to an unruly German tourist and doesn't see me. I hope she finds it later and it makes her happy.

★

The Plan is running smoothly. Everything is on track. Got the money, got absolution, made the bathroom attendant's day, confessed. Now the dentist awaits. Time to eradicate the crippling jaw pain. But how to get there? The Upper East Side is so out of the way they should just call it another borough. I go over all my transportation options and conclude that it would be easiest to walk. Fifteen blocks in, and my wrist is about to break from the weight of the metal case. And my shoulders are killing me; two million dollars weighs a ton. For the first time since I've lived in the city, I am afraid of being mugged. I feel like I have a target painted on my back. Every guy I pass is eyeballing me, wondering, I'm sure, what's in my knapsack. Paranoia is coursing through my veins and making me clench my teeth.

I finally reach the dentist's office. My jaw is throbbing, my back is aching, I'm sweaty and basically disgusting. I reach out to push the elevator button and get a whiff of my own BO. All I want to do is get home and shower. The receptionist greets me with a nod. Even she eyeballs the silver case.

"I love that briefcase."

"Do you want it?"

"Are you serious?"

"Sure. I'm sick of it." I hand it over.

"Wow, it's heavy." She puts it under her desk. She looks pleased, as if it's some windfall. After a moment she sends me in. I heave my knapsack into the corner, get into the chair, and then the same horrid hygienist from last time enters, wielding her floss.

"I'm here to get my splint—"

"Well, a quick floss never hurts."

"I don't need a floss—"

"I insist. You're in my chair, you get a floss."

The next thing I know, she's all over me. It's like something out of *Marathon Man*. I'm squirming in the chair, and she's jamming floss between my teeth. Who does she think she is? And more than that, what does she have against me? My persecution complex is raging. I hate authority; I realize I could never work in corporate America. I have no choice but to return to music. I can't live like this; I can't breathe! She pulls out the floss and shoves it near my nose.

"Smell it."

I recoil.

"Smell it!"

"Thanks, Joni; I'll take it from here."

I hear the dentist, her voice like an angel from heaven. And

Joni leaves, muttering, "Her gums are awful. My guess is within seven years, all her teeth are going to fall out. . . ." Judy the dentist sits down and hands me my splint. It's amazingly small, barely the size of a retainer. Nothing but a cheap piece of plastic with a little metal insert. It could cost no more than ten bucks to make, and I've paid $650. This injustice, on top of the floss assault, is simply too much to bear. I feel a rant percolating. I'm going to tell Judy the dentist that I'm on to the little racket she's got going. I'm going to tell her that Joni the hygienist is a horrible person; I'm going to demand that her license be revoked. I'm going to demand a formal apology.

"Joni is kinda mean." This is the best I can do.

"She's harmless. She just wants people to floss."

"She told me that no one would marry me, much less have children with me, if I didn't start flossing."

"That's nothing; she told a guy last week that the plaque was going to shrink his penis."

"Why does she do that?"

"She takes her job very seriously."

I snort.

"She wants people to floss; we all want people to floss. Joni gets results. Let me ask you something. Since you were here last week, have you flossed?"

"Twice a day. Religiously."

"Then her work is done."

Judy shoves the splint into my mouth, rendering me mute. It may look small, but it doesn't feel small. She yanks it out of my mouth. She drills it, files it, sticks it back in my mouth and has me bite down on small pieces of black paper, which feel like chalk. In fifteen minutes I'm done and out the door, splint in my mouth, two million bucks on my back. I stand on the corner for a moment. Everything is going so smoothly. I decide I should check my machine, make sure Lil hasn't called and changed all the plans. I feel around in my pockets, thinking it will be ironic if I don't have a quarter, but I have one. I dial up my number and listen. There is a message.

"Hey, Parker, this is Kim from the location office. We're on lunch right now, but we'll be heading over in about thirty minutes for blocking and rehearsal. Any problems please call my office, 212-555–4545."

Thirty minutes? What day *is* today? I run to the newsstand and look at a paper. Thursday late edition. It's Thursday. They're not supposed to come until Friday. I haven't even showered, much less double conditioned, and it's not like I can reschedule Lil and her kidnappers. This was not The Plan!

I'm sweating profusely, creating a veritable greenhouse effect over my entire body. Pores are opening, whiteheads are emerging, hair is frizzing, stenches are rising. I fumble for another quarter. Dial up Kim's number.

"Production?"

"Can I speak to Kim? This is Parker Grey, they're using my apartment today—"

"Just a sec . . ."

I'm on hold for what seems like an eternity.

"This is Kim. Is there a problem?"

"Well. When we spoke, you told me you guys were coming on Friday."

"No way! I said *Thursday*. I specifically said Thursday. I even have it here in my notes, your name with Thursday circled."

I don't see how I could've made this mistake. She's the one juggling locations; all I had to remember was Thursday. *She* screwed up.

"Is this going to be a problem? Because if this is going to be a problem, we're going to have to figure something out, because I specifically said Thursday. I would *never* screw up something like that—"

I can see arguing isn't going to do any good. Clearly, they're not going to switch days. "No, it's not a problem; I just thought it was going to be Friday. I'm uptown right now; I had a dental emergency. I can be back in about forty-five minutes."

"They'll be there in thirty."

"I'll do the best I can."

"I'll send someone to pick you up. Where are you?"

"I'm on the Upper East Side. By the time they get here, it won't be worth it. I'll hop a train." Something I didn't really want to do, considering the giant lump of cash I have strapped to my back.

"Hurry! I'll tell the AD to stall for a few minutes; they have to make a company move; hopefully that'll take a little longer than expected."

She's so frantic, she's making me frantic. I have no idea what the AD is. I'm thinking it's some kind of lawyer. Thirty minutes! The gods are working against me; they don't even want me to smell good for M. He's going to see me like this and throw me back in the water! I'm grinding my teeth so hard, the splint goes flying out of my mouth and lands in a dirty puddle. Things are going from bad to worse. I fish it out with my hand, shove it in my pocket, and head into the 6 train.

★

"Are you Parker?!"

"I am!"

A very stressed-out woman on the front steps of my building is yelling down the block to me. I assume this is Kim. She waits for me to get to the stairs. When I get there, she doesn't smile. "We're going to need you to let us in."

I feel like I'm in trouble. I fumble for my keys and open up the door. Kim and I rush up the stairs. We're joined by Kent. Kent is the AD. I learn that AD means assistant director. I assume he's a very important person. He's wearing a giant headset; it reminds me of the one John Williams wore when he was conducting at the '84 Olympics.

"Is there an elevator?!!"

"No."

"Christ!!!"

"Sorry! I didn't know!" I have no idea why I'm apologizing.

"It's *fine*. But we're going to have to factor that into first team."

Another girl with a headset and a metal notebook joins us. All this, and we're not even to the second floor. Kent is rattling off orders. I feel like we're going to storm Normandy.

"Get Lone Wolf on the phone. Tell him we won't need him until eight. Call his driver; make sure we get confirmation from both of them. Let hair and makeup know that we'll be lighting, and they should break away."

I'm at the door, and Kent's stress and anxiety is radiating into me. He's still talking into his headset. "I need stand-ins! I want to start blocking! Does anyone have a twenty on the director, and we're gonna need art department up here!"

The minute I open the door, my apartment is overrun by guys carrying vast amounts of equipment. I head into my bedroom, running away from all these people. I hide the knapsack in the back of my closet and cover it with as much crap as I can. Losing the money at this point would just be ridiculous. I sit down on my bed. I'm exhausted, and there's still a long night ahead of me. This wasn't how it was supposed to go down. My room seems like a foreign space to me. I haven't slept in here since Lil's been gone. It's all so bare and cell-like. I've been living like this for over six months. A mattress on the floor, a lamp on a milk crate, and a half-finished painting of a Hindu woman, leaning against the wall. I've had this painting all my life. My mother painted it before I was born but stopped midway, because she realized that the Hindu woman's face was the face of her dead mother. I found it when I was little, and I've always kept it with me. My way of remembering a woman I never knew.

"*Parker!*"

I look up and realize that Kim has been calling my name.

"We need you to come out here."

I follow like a repentant child, out into the living room,

where five people I've never met are staring up at the Color-form wall. Then a guy wearing skinny pants and a T-shirt enters. He's sort of goofy looking, with big, black-framed eyeglasses. There's an air about him, as if he's not all in this world.

"I'm Steven."

"Hi. I'm Parker."

Kent leans over to me. "Steven is our director."

He says it with such reverence, as if I'm supposed to genuflect. Steven ignores him. He's very focused. I admire that in people.

"Did you do this?"

"Yeah."

"Tell me about it."

I'd like to have something really intelligent to say, but I don't. The truth is, I don't know why I did it. I'm amazed at how good it looks. I'm amazed that I did it at all. "I guess, I just wanted to create something. And I started it, and it just took on a life of its own." Which is all true. I look at Steven for a response, but he's staring at it, nodding to himself. Then he looks at me.

"Thank you for creating this."

He's so earnest about it. I listen for affectation but there is none. Another guy holds a light meter up to it. "It's gonna look beautiful, Steven." Steven nods again, his head in the clouds.

Kent leans in, so desperate to be his favorite. "He was right about this place." Steven looks up at the Smith chandelier. "This is wild. Yours, too?"

"Yeah. It's just a connector really, between the Colorform wall and the graffiti wall. I needed some motion. I don't know." I sound like an idiot. But Steven remains thoughtful.

"I want to lower the chandelier so it's in frame. But we'll be careful with it."

Smith's letterhead will be in the picture, but at this point, who cares.

"And this is just tremendous. Bonnie Cashin had one just like it in her apartment."

"You knew her?"

"Briefly."

I'm about to ask Steven about her. I want to tell him all about my pocket purses and how it's a tribute to her and how Bonnie Cashin is one of my heroes. But jealous Kent butts his nose in. "Do you want me to bring everyone up for rehearsal?" Steven heads off, saying, "Give me five minutes." He doesn't bother to say good-bye or thanks or anything, and in an instant my apartment is obliterated by cables and lights and cameras. There's even a table set up in the hallway with food on it. I see one of Kent's minions asking Stockbroker Guy to not touch the croissants.

★

I haven't even showered today. And now M is on his way up for rehearsal. I head into the bathroom and jam the stepladder against the door. I have about a minute and a half to whip off my clothes and clean myself with a washcloth. I'm being punished for threatening to double condition my hair. Now I can't even wash it. I stick my leg in the sink and shave it fast.

I cut myself in the process, but I don't care. I do the other leg and then I hit the pits. One quick whack and I'm smooth as a wet duck. I splash water all over my body, trying to get the vital parts before I pull on a pair of blue capris that have been lying on the floor for a week. Luckily, they're not wrinkled. Then I fish through the laundry for my blue halter top that fits so perfectly, I'm certain it was sewn specifically for me. I spray it with deodorant, shake it off, and put it on. I don't bother with makeup. I keep thinking of Trudy. Totally natural, totally yourself. I rub some Badescu lotion on my arms to make them shine and swack some Vaseline across my lips. They key word to this look is *shine*. Then I give my hair a shake. It actually doesn't look that bad. The frizz has died down, and now it's just kind of wavy.

"Let's get ready for rehearsal, people! Let's lock it up!"

I can hear Kent's big mouth booming. I step out, my heart pounding. This is it. The moment I've been waiting for. I look for M across the room. I've waited oceans of time for this. . . .

But I don't see M; I see some tall guy with dark hair. He's got a similar build, but other than that, there's no resemblance. He's reading lines. His performance is atrocious. Do they not see that this guy is awful? That he is not M? I turn and see a guy; he's messing around with a camera. "Isn't M in this movie?"

"He is. Yeah—"

"Then who's that guy?" I feel like La Femme, in the movie version, when she thinks she's dead and she's not sure if she's in heaven or not. She turns to Bob and says, "Mister, is this heaven or what?"

"That's the stand-in. He's just here so we can set marks for lighting. The actors don't come until later."

I could hug him. M is coming. But not until later. Later? Later is not good. Later, I will not be here. I want to ask him another question, but I think that if I do, I will look pathetic. Instead, I sit down on an apple box, that's what I hear the man call it. I just sit there and watch and wait.

★

Two hours later, and they're still setting up. This is about as exciting as watching paint dry. I spot Kim in the corner; she's eating a croissant. I think that with her thunderous thighs, Kim should lay off the croissants. I really don't want to ask her about M because I don't want to come off like a fan, but I've got so much to do and this is my only chance. I can't reschedule Lil. I sidle up to her. I try to be casual. I tell myself, *You're in character and your character could give a shit about all this.* Which in a way is sort of true. "When do you think they're going to start shooting?"

"Who knows? At this rate, I'd say not until at least ten-thirty."

I want to know when M is coming. Is he en route? Is he in the vicinity? Where is he? But I can't ask. I just feel too stupid. She sees that I have a pack of smokes on the table.

"They yours?"

"Yeah, you want one?"

"That'd be great."

Bonding over smoking. Always a good sign. Now we're two smokers, sharing a common wretched addiction. I'm psyched. I'm in. We'll light up, and she'll start telling me all about her life. Like two alcoholics. I hand her the pack, but she turns up her nose.

"I thought they were menthol."

Menthol. The gap that divides. I look at her with disgust. Menthols are revolting. She looks at me with equal disdain. I will not be getting any more information out of her tonight. And so I'm stuck.

What would Parker Grey do?

Parker would stick to The Plan. She would never go out of her way for any guy. Even M. She would go to the bar, stash the credit-card money, and tip off the FBI. And so I remove thirty-five thousand dollars from the knapsack, less the two hundred that I gave to the bathroom attendant, and stick it inside a small makeup bag. The money will be safer in the bar. If anything goes wrong, no one will look for it there.

I know this because Parker Grey knows this, and I am Parker Grey.

TWENTY-SIX

The bar is busy for a Thursday night. Jose, the cook, is throwing slabs of halibut into the fryer. Next to him, his cousin Jesus, with the clubfoot and the fierce wandering eye, is cutting potatoes for fries. Jesus sees me come into the kitchen and sticks his tongue out. "Hey baby, come over here and I show you a good time with my tongue."

We should all have Jesus' inflated sense of self . . .

Down in the cellar I find the old Schaefer beer sign, lean it over, and see that Smith's letters are still safe and sound. I grab them, and in their place I stash the money.

"Parker?"

I jump up and smash my head on the low ceiling. "Shit!" The pain runs through my body like an electric current. *Fuck* . . .

"Parker, what are you doing down here?"

I hold my head, as if it's going to quell the pain everywhere else. "I have to put something in a safe place."

"What are you mixed up in, Parker?"

"I'm not mixed up in anything, Tom; I just need to store something."

Tommy knows I'm bullshitting. I've got a very small window to figure something out. I don't want to lie, but I have no choice. "Uncle Bill . . ." As in Big Bill Grey, the Westie. Who I am now officially related to. "He asked me to put something in a safe place for him."

Tommy looks at me. I tell myself to believe with every inch of my body what I'm saying. Believe the lie. Believe it. Embrace it. He's still staring at me. I stare right back. We're like two samurai in the rain. Until it breaks.

"Whatever you need to do, Parker."

I've won.

"Just no body parts."

Body parts? What does he take me for? "Don't worry, it's nothing like that." *It's just kidnapping, extortion, and bribery.*

"Wait 'til I go up; I don't want to see anything."

I go for broke. "Tommy, this is just between us, right? My uncle'd be pissed if he knew I . . ." I don't even have to finish the sentence.

"Do what you have to do, Parker. When you're done, come in the back room. I've got the machine; we'll sing a few songs."

"I don't know. I've got a bunch of stuff I have to do—"

"Parker, you still work for me. Get your ass up there and

sing a few goddamn songs. Make a miserable fuck like me happy." He laughs that phlegm-rattling laugh of his and heads back up the ladder.

★

Tommy has invited half the bar into the back room. It's all very flattering, but I don't have time to do the entire set of eighties pop hits that he's got lined up for me.

"You can't believe this girl's voice. Fucking amazing. And she's wasting her time in fucking journalism school."

"Law school."

"Whatever."

I begin to think maybe people aren't paying attention to half the stuff that I say. Tommy hands me the mike. "But . . ."

"Shut up and sing."

Now I know how Elvis felt. I get to work, the Colonel by my side pointing at the lyrics of an old Tom Waits song that found its way into the thankless hands of Scandal. The words are great. Tom Waits is a tortured genius. Tommy forces a second song on me, and I sing it. In another time and another place, this would be enjoyable. But not tonight. The clock on the wall says that it's ten of ten, and I'm sweating, which means hair frizz is impending. After the third song, I draw the line. I can't do this. Not now. And I feel guilty, like I'm letting Tommy down. Now I understand why Elvis could never shake the Colonel. "I've got to go."

"Where the fuck do you have to go?"

"I have a date."

"A date?! Who's the creepy cocksucker?"

"Just a guy."

"I hope he's better than the last a-hole you were with."

"When did you see him?"

"I see everything, Parker. He was a real asshole."

He was an asshole, and I was a fool. I try to hand him back the mike. He won't take it.

"Besides, what kind of date happens at ten at night? The guy can't even take you to dinner."

"Tommy, I gotta go!"

"Well," he takes the mike, "keep your eyes open and your legs shut!"

He's still hollering advice after me, but I'm halfway out the door.

★

A few blocks away, I call the bar from a pay phone. I cover the receiver with my hand. I'm nervous because this time is for real. And this time, I know the FBI is really listening.

"Bar Sixty."

It's Margaret. I think I might burst out laughing, but then I think of Lil, and I pull it together. I put on a weird, creepy voice. "The Toxic Avengers are going to strike again." There's a pause. Margaret is so bored. I feel it through the lines. But I also know that Margaret is irate, and she'll engage me, which is good.

"Who is this?"

"I'm with the Toxic Avengers, and we're going to blow up a plant tomorrow night."

"What makes you think I give a shit?"

Margaret is so great.

"We're telling the world. We're fighting the corporate giants who think they can suck the life out of the ecosystem and not pay. Tomorrow night, J. G. Wendeborn is going to pay—"

"Go fuck yourself."

Margaret hangs up. I check my watch, five of ten. I pull out a moist towelette that I swiped from the kitchen and wipe the phone down. No prints.

★

Back at my apartment, unbelievably, they're still lighting. It's roasting, the pace is feverish, and the bizarro M is still standing exactly where he was when I left. He looks really bored. It's now ten o'clock, and I'm supposed to be at the Port Authority doing a walkabout, but instead, I'm here waiting for M, and he's nowhere to be seen. Then I spot some guy with a headset, one of Kent's minions, playing Humphrey.

The fucking nerve.

That's *my* Humphrey. He's been with me for ten years. I can treat him like shit, but I will not tolerate strange hands groping his body. I head over. I try to remain calm, but I'm crazed inside because the truth is, I love Humphrey, and I can't bear the thought of anything happening to him. That and the fact that he's a ten-thousand-dollar instrument. "Could you *not* play that?"

There are three of them. They all turn and look at me. I'm sure I'm coming off like a giant bitch, but the reality is, I'm just being honest. I don't want them touching him.

"Sure, sorry. It's a nice guitar." He hands it back to me. "You play?"

I tell myself to calm down. If I get stressed, the sweat will start, and I will be frizzing before I know it. "Yeah. I do."

Another one of the guys tells me he likes the walls. "Great place. It's really amazing."

"Thanks."

"Play us something."

I hate this. Like I'm a trained seal. "I don't know . . ."

"Anything. Come on! Can't you play?"

This always annoys me. First they want you to perform on command, and then when you don't, they accuse you of not being able to play. No one tells painters to do a little drawing. They never tell dancers to do a little jig in the middle of the room, or actors to just bust out into a scene. I hate music without context. I hate it because it's false, and it's not what music is about. Music is about connecting, it's about expression, it's about revealing yourself. It's not about proving to some stranger that you can move your fingers across the strings fast. But still, my ego rages. I could play something. It's been six months, but I could. I could play them something that would make their heads spin. I could play arpeggios at warp speed; I could play an old flamenco song. Very percussive, very sexy.

It would impress them.

But I don't want to impress anyone. I spent years trying to impress people, and it just made me miserable. I put Humphrey back on his stand and move him to the corner, away from the lights. The guys look at me. They think I can't

play, but I no longer care. It's ten-thirty. I can't wait a moment longer. I have to save Lil. I pull the knapsack with the
ransom money out of my closet and head out. I tell Kim I'm
leaving. They can lock up when they're done.

"Cool, we'll get you a check for the apartment."

★

I head down the steps and I almost miss him. He is coming
up, flanked by one of Kent's minions. Her walkie-talkie is
chattering away. When I do see him, he's nearly past me. And
all I notice are those eyes. Those dark, brooding eyes. They
stare at me, almost through me. As if he's speaking to me but
without words. But I keep going. Because the show must go
on.

Yet in the moment that it takes for my foot to hit the steps,
I think about everything. How M asked for me in the bar,
how Trudy said I can't be afraid of happiness, how lonely I've
been, how I've thrown everything away. I think about the last
six months, and the four years before that, and the twenty before that. I think about how I've been searching, my whole
life it seems, for something to make sense. And that something, at least part of that something, is walking past me on
the steps. And in the moment that it takes my foot to hit the
next stair, I realize that at the very least, I have to turn back
because if I don't, I'll disappear. And so I turn. And as I turn,
I expect nothing.

Because all the expectation is in the turn itself.

And when I look back, he's there, looking right back at me.
Kent's minion is still by his side. And from the looks of it,

she's not happy. She speaks into her headset. "First team is stepping onto set."

First team is not stepping onto set. He's standing on the stairs looking at me.

"Where are you going?"

He says it with such desperation, like La Femme when she didn't know if she was dead or not. Like me, asking the cameraman if M was in the movie. All of this is lost on Kent's minion. "They're ready for you."

He doesn't even look at her. "I'll be right in."

She doesn't move. He turns; this time it's more forceful. *"I'll be right in."*

She exhales loudly. I suppose she gets in trouble for this kind of thing. But she heads inside anyway. And here we are, standing in the stairway.

Just staring at one another.

I keep waiting for him to say something, and I think it's the same for him. But I don't know where to begin. And then he goes first. "I don't want you to go."

I don't understand what's happening. I haven't been given the script. I don't know what my next line should be. But he's here, and he doesn't want me to go. It takes every ounce of energy just to open my mouth. "I have to go. My friend's in trouble." Two simple sentences, and both of them honest. "She's been kidnapped, and I have to drop off the ransom money or else, well, or else they're going to kill her." I've said it. There it is. And it's not so bad. I unzip the knapsack a little so he can see all the cash in there.

"Will you be okay?" He looks genuinely worried.

"Oh yeah, just a bunch of stupid Eco-Rectifiers, but I'm dealing with them as well." Simple, fluid, effortless, and without fear. If he throws me back in, I'll swim away and be fine. "More than anything, I'd like to talk with you. It's just bad timing, I guess."

I see the hint of a smile in his eyes. "I'll wait."

And just like that it's settled. He'll wait.

TWENTY-SEVEN

The train ride takes about eight minutes. I push through the turnstile, past the newsstand where Lil once dared me to buy a copy of *Big Butt* magazine. The surly guy refused to sell it to me. "*Big Butt* sold out." That's all he said. Then he waved me off dismissively, although it was obvious that he was lying. We could see the issues behind the counter. Lil ranted for a week that she was going to sue for discrimination. Then she met Smith at an endowment reception and forgot all about it.

Inside the Port Authority, the smell of Pine Sol mixed with urine permeates the air. There's a single janitor mopping. I take an escalator up to the third floor, where the New Jersey Transit buses are. Past the elevators, I see a few drivers sitting in the dispatch office sipping coffee out of white paper cups.

Only one more run tonight. The buses stop at midnight. Back when I lived at home, I used to sprint to catch the eleven-forty-five, because missing it meant sleeping on the floor with a bunch of runaways in the old building next door and incurring the wrath of my mother. Even back then, all I ever did was make her worry. I still have fifteen minutes. I guess there really was no reason to come earlier. What was I going to see? Buses, homeless people, pigeons.

The place is deserted enough that no one notices when I head out the door marked 99, and into the garage itself. I stay on the walkway. Careful, alert, guarded. Two million on my back, this is no time to get mugged. But there's no one around. We may as well have met at the piers. The walkway leads to the other gates. I follow it, passing them, 100, 101, 102. . . . Each with its own glass-enclosed waiting area. I'm supposed to meet them at gate 108. I look ahead and see that I'm the first to have arrived, and instantly, I don't like it. If I wait in the gate, I'm going to look like a sitting duck. I need to make more of an impression. I need to make an entrance. Then I hear a bus approaching. These drivers fly through the garage like they're behind the wheel of a Maserati. The driver nearly jumps the curb before he parks in slot 106. He leaves his bus idling. Then he heads inside for what I imagine to be a cup of bad coffee and conversation. The bus is alone and unattended. I climb inside.

The windows are tinted, and from this inside vantage point, the view of the garage and gate 108 is panoramic. I've read enough Sun Tzu to know that this is a good thing. The only foreseeable glitch is if the driver comes back out and drives away. It's nearly 11:30. The buses run fifteen minutes before and fifteen after. If they're on time, I'll be okay. My hands are trembling slightly, which is funny because I don't feel scared. I just want to see Lil. I've almost forgotten what it's like to have her around.

Then I see them. They're heading into the garage from the same door I came through. I watch through the tinted window. I see Lil. She's talking to them. Gesticulating wildly, which is something she does when she's trying to make a point. I wonder what she's saying. There are three of them with her. All guys. All dressed alike in crappy T-shirts and cargo pants. And all with shaved heads. The guy next to Lil must be Shipherd. He's sinewy. The two guys with him, one's very tall, the other very short. The juxtaposition is almost comical. Shipherd and his crack team, Frick and Frack, making the world safe for yellow-shafted flickers.

But the closer they get, the more uncertain I become. Frick and Frack look slightly menacing, and suddenly I'm not sure how to play this. The immortal words of General Patton ring through my ears: "When you get there, you'll know what to do." But I don't. I should probably get off this bus, but I don't want to do anything to scare them. What if they have guns or bombs? What if Lil freaks out and tries to shoot me? I hear their voices as they come closer. Lil's ranting.

"The fat Elvis *totally* should have been given the stamp!"

"I don't know, the skinny Elvis was so much hipper with his blue suede shoes and all."

"Shipherd! What are you talking about? Are you a fucking anticorporate hero or not?"

"I'm just saying fat Elvis was, you know . . . lame . . . with the karate and all."

"Fat Elvis is the *embodiment* of all that is good and all that is bad with America and the American Dream!"

Lil wrote a master's thesis on Elvis. *The Vilification of the American Dream: Elvis as Demon and Father Figure.* All she did to write it was watch *Viva Las Vegas* about a hundred times. She won an award for it.

". . . The American Dream is not about achievement, it's about the *journey*. And once Elvis arrived, there was nothing. No structure, no internal integrity, no code of honor. There was only gloss, nothing else. And he had no skills to deal with it, and so he became corrupted. He fell for all of us. He died for our sins as a *society*."

I've been in bars with Lil, late at night, when she's had this conversation with perfect strangers. I know the ins and outs of the Fat Elvis vs. the Skinny Elvis debate, and I, too, believe that it should have been the bloated, bejeweled Elvis, sweating in Honolulu, on that stamp. And then Lil looks straight at me. Apparently, the bus windows aren't as tinted as they appear to be from the inside. I duck down. My heart pounding so fast I feel like a hummingbird or maybe a yellow-shafted flicker. *Do something, do anything. Move.* I feel the knapsack in my clenched hand. *Bring them the money. Yes! Bring out the money!* Money in hand, I head down the aisle.

And then I hit the deck.

Because Lil's on the bus, in the driver's seat, and she's just slammed the door shut. The Toxic Avengers are outside, banging on the door, not happy at all. And I'm crouched down in the aisle, in plain sight, afraid to move. Afraid that I might frighten her. But she's *seen* me. She looked right at me. She *knows* I'm here.

"Fucking moron is going to argue with *me* about Elvis!"

"Lil?"

She messes with the stick shift, sending the bus lurching forward and me with it. I go flying, sliding down the aisle face first. I slam up against the front console as the knapsack tumbles out of my hands and into the stairwell. I can't get my bearings, and I see Shipherd, looking like a rabid dog, jamming his sinewy forearm against the door, trying desperately to get the knapsack. I dive down the stairwell, my feet clinging to the metal brackets that hold the driver's seat. I'm not even thinking at this point. It's all very visceral. I'm going for the bag. I'm not letting them walk away with the money. This is my show, and they're not going to get away with this. Bad guys don't walk away with two million cash.

Now Frick and Frack are in the act, grimacing, using all their strength to pry open the double doors. And Shipherd's arm is through; he's pawing at me, groping wildly, but I won't give him the bag. I won't let go. He's digging his hand into my arm. The pain is horrendous, but I won't let go. "Get us outta here, Lil!"

"I'm trying!"

I twist Shipherd's finger. Hard. Violent. I've hurt him. Something I didn't think I had in me. But it's self-preservation. I pull the bag close to me, jam my foot against the door, using all my strength to offset Frick and Frack on the other side. Finally, Lil shoves the bus into reverse. Shipherd's arm is stuck, and he's jogging to keep up, half trying to get his arm out, half trying to get the bag. I look at his hand. His nails are dirty. It seems like the hand I'm smacking away and the guy jogging on the other side of the door are two totally separate entities. Lil downshifts, the speed sends Shipherd to the ground.

"You are dead! Totally dead, Chloe!"

"Why is he calling you Chloe?!"

"He thinks that's my name!"

I forgot. They think she's Smith's daughter. Lil kicks the bus into another gear. The grinding is awful, but we begin to move faster. "Parker!!! How the fuck are you?!" I pull myself up from the stairwell and hang on to the pole next to her. In the rearview mirror I see Shipherd, Frick, and Frack running after us. Lil isn't exactly Parnelli. "You've got to speed up; we're going too slow!"

"I can't find the right gear!"

As Lil's grinding gears, trying to get her footing, I realize we're just going around in circles. "I thought you had Stockholm syndrome," I say, as I look out the back window. The three goons are getting frustrated; they seem to be conferring among themselves. What are they plotting?

Lil laughs. The one with no sound. The one when something really cracks her up. "That's hilarious. You didn't get it?"

"Get what?"

"I was faking it! Totally faking it."

"So you're not upset about the yellow-shafted flickers, and

you don't think Smith is your father? You're not in love with that neo-Nazi?"

"No!!!!"

I can't believe I fell for it. And yet it all makes sense.

"It was a role. Nothing more."

Of course.

"I was using him, tricking him. It was very empowering."

We've just missed the ramp to get out. This isn't good. We have two million dollars and three goons on our tail. "Lil, we've got to get the ramp!" She nods, turns the bus in the right direction. She knows the Port Authority about as well as I do, from back in the day. "By the way, Parker, your hair looks *amazing*."

It's so good to have Lil back. "I didn't have time to wash it."

"It looks great."

"So, all this time you were okay?"

"I swear, Parker, I thought you'd know. You figured everything else out."

"I didn't. I was worried."

"Never worry about me, Parker. No one fucks with me."

"I thought you had become a Toxic Avenger. I thought you were going to blow up Smith's factory." It's all such a relief.

"Did you tell Smith?"

"No, I did better; I tipped off the papers and the FBI."

"The FBI?!"

"The phone at the bar is tapped."

"No shit!" Lil is cracking up. "You are so fucking *brilliant*, Parker."

She takes the ramp fast, and in a moment we're crossing Forty-second Street and heading down Eleventh Avenue. It dawns on me that we're stealing a bus when—*bammmm!*— we lurch forward in a bad way. I look behind us and see Shipherd and company in another New Jersey Transit bus. They are going to ram us again. I quickly brace myself behind a seat. Lil sees him. Shakes her head. Irritated. But says nothing.

Bammm! He slams into us hard. The front of the bus is flat; it makes for a nice clean bump, but it doesn't do much damage. The key is to keep the body braced. My head back, my feet pushing against the seat in front of me.

"How did Smith take it all?"

"I don't know. He's weird. Did you know he's into gay porn?"

"I know."

"You know?"

"Yeah. He didn't drag you to that stupid theater, did he?"

"You know about the gay porn!?"

"Yeah, it's his thing. Frankly, I've always wanted to have a threesome with two guys, so his perversion suited me. Sort of like the way guys don't mind if their girlfriends sleep with other girls."

You learn something new about your friends every day.

Shipherd tries to sideswipe us, but Lil cuts him off. We scrape the side of his bus. Metal crunches, sparks fly. And we race down Eleventh Avenue, the bus going so fast it feels like a boat.

"Mother fucker, Chloe! You're one of us!" Shipherd screams at Lil through the open door of his bus. He can't understand how Chloe can do this to him. But this is not Chloe. This is Lil. If he had looked close enough, he would have seen it. The hidden always becomes exposed. Like an underpainting emerging from the coat of paint covering it, revealing itself to the viewer.

"Sorry!? Can't hear you!"

Shipherd is freaking out. But not Lil; she remains calm. We should all have her poise. He sideswipes us again, and I'm hanging on so tight my body is starting to ache. But I'm more numbed by the fact that there isn't a single cop in sight. All I know for sure is that I'm the only girl in the city, and probably in the world, who's having a chase in a bus at this very moment. Besides Lil, that is.

We're moving so fast the city is a blur. An impression of itself. The night hangs low, as if there's no sky. Maybe it's because the buildings are so high, but it seems as if there's nothing but darkness and light. And only the clusters of buildings, with their glowing windows, bear witness to this, the most absurd of chases. Inside them, the faceless live, breathe, and sleep. Inside, the futons, the Chinese take-out containers, the remotes lost behind sofa cushions. The bathrooms out of toilet paper, a wad of napkins shoved into the space where the toilet paper should be. The dirty clothes, the messy beds. The huddled masses.

"Parker, hang on!!!" Lil slams the brakes. The bus screams as if it's in pain. We swerve. I look out and see Shipherd coming straight for us, like a kamikaze bus driver from hell. And what amazes me most is not the level of anger that I can see racing across his pinched, contorted face but rather the fact that he doesn't seem to care that he's about to careen directly into us. Not only does he have zero regard for Lil and me, he also has no regard for himself. Every muscle in my body begins to collapse slowly, in anticipation of the impact. It's as if I'm doing my body the courtesy of falling to pieces before it has to. And then all at once, I'm out of control.

I can't tell if we've been hit, but my body is going one way and my arms are going another, and my brain says to stand up, but I can't. I'm pinned in a seat, my legs up in the air like a giant V, and I realize we're spinning. I see the streetlights coming and going, then coming again. And the fear of impact keeps me lucid. I struggle against the centrifugal force of it all, trying desperately to pull myself up.

We jerk to a stop, and I wait for the crash, the crunch, the *ugh,* as I smash my head and fall down. There's a silence, and I wait inside it. And then comes the sound. A terrible, plaintive screech. It's the sound of metal crunching. The sound of impact. I cling to myself, my own desperate savior. But it's not us. It's not us at all.

"Parker?! You okay?"

I fumble for the window, my body confused and disoriented. I see Shipherd's bus, across the street. Slammed into a pole. I look around, there's traffic on the street, but no one seems to care; they're all just going around us, and we're in the middle lane. And we're okay. But the other bus is not, or so it seems. But then I see Shipherd and Frick and Frack stumble out. They're alive. Bloody but alive.

Lil throws our bus into gear and turns down the street. In New York, apparently, you can have a high-speed chase with another bus down a main avenue, and not a single cop will show up. Not a single driver will honk a horn, not a single pedestrian will stop to call 911. It's our blessing, I suppose, and for bystanders, a curse. I want off of this scrap heap, but Lil's settling in.

"I've been locked up with those nut jobs for ten days now. Let me drive for a minute."

I don't argue with her. Whether she wants to admit it or not, she's been through a trauma. I sit down in the front seat and rest my feet on the stairwell wall. Just breathe. The rest will take care of itself. I look at Lil; she's so confident. "Were you scared?"

"Not really. Well, that's not true. I was a little scared, mostly because they were just so stupid."

"Could you have left?"

"No, definitely not. They made that clear, and there was always one of them watching."

"Where were you?"

"I don't know. I couldn't tell; the windows were blacked out." She shrugs it off. For Lil, it's pretty much over.

I look out the window. I love the city at night. I think of my mother, how she used to drive us around at night, just to do something. Just to get out of the house. She used to say it was a cheap date. And it had to be, because she didn't have a dime back then. All of us piled inside her beat-up Chevette, driving around the city looking in other people's windows. I feel a general sense of happiness come over me, but I can't place it. It's as if it's a secret that my mind doesn't want to let me in on.

And then, of course, I remember.

M.

"So how are you? You're all in your head."

"What?"

"You're doing that hand thing. You do it when you're zoning out." She makes a funny movement with her hand.

"Do I do that?"

"Constantly. You look like a cat."

Funny what you don't know about yourself. "M's at the apartment."

"Our apartment?"

"Yeah. He's waiting there. . . ."

"Your M . . . What's he doing there?!"

"I'm not a hundred percent sure how it all happened, but he's filming a movie, and they're using the apartment, and he's there and . . . he's been at the bar asking about me."

"Jesus Christ, Parker, if I'd known, we could've done this tomorrow night. I'm sooo sorry. Fuck. Parker. I'm totally screwing this up for you. You should've said something on the phone."

"I didn't know then. It just sort of happened. Besides, I didn't want to be, you know, selfish."

"Fuck that. For once in your life, be selfish! There's nothing wrong with it." Lil turns onto Canal Street.

"What are you doing?"

"I'm getting you home. Then I'll ditch the bus and stay at my dad's for the night."

The knapsack is wedged between two seats. I yank it out. "What are we gonna do with all this money?"

"Take it home with you tonight. We're gonna split it."

"What if it's marked?"

"Please. Smith's not in the mob. He doesn't mark his money."

"I feel morally conflicted."

"Why?"

"Because I already bilked him out of thirty-five grand to pay off my credit-card bills."

Lil pounds the steering wheel, she's laughing so hard. Even I have to crack up.

"I love it! Well, now you've got one million, and you're debt free."

"You sure?"

"Who'll know?"

She's right. No one will ever know. Smith's not going to talk, Shipherd's not going to bitch to anyone.

"Parker, it's pocket change for Smith. I wouldn't even have considered it, but the empty suitcase. That was a real kick in the teeth."

I imagine it was. For me too. But Lil senses lingering conflict.

"Do bad things, Parker. Do bad things, like I always say, and the good karma will come back your way. Gotta send out your negative energy to get back the positive energy. It's yin and yang. We are both good and bad. We're complex creatures. You can't integrate them all; you just accept them all. And in doing so, you become, you know, without sounding like an asshole, you become *whole*."

I love that Lil can completely bastardize an entire school of philosophy to meet her own needs. But she has a point. "I'm glad you're back, Lil."

"So am I."

Lil turns onto Varick Street. Another block and I'm home.

TWENTY-EIGHT

I'm struck by how empty the apartment seems. All those people, and now there are none. Yet their presence looms; I can feel the room reeling. The toilet flushes. I turn, my heart beating wildly. But it's the location scout, carrying a bag of trash. I recognize him from the other night. Only now he's got two big black eyes and a bandage over his nose. I did this to him, and he has no idea. I smile at him as he leaves. My apology hidden in the smile.

Location Scout Guy shuts the door, and all that's left is me. My heart slows and dies a little bit. I think of the thousand little deaths that came before it. I suppose I just want things too badly. I long for things too much. And then they don't happen. And now I'm back in the water. But I can still swim.

"I was afraid you weren't coming back."

I turn and see him sitting in the window seat. An electrical current brings me back to life. My heart quickens. "There were . . . ahhhh . . . complications. . . ." I don't know how else to describe it. "Bus chase" sounds like an absurd lie.

"Your friend is all right?"

"She's fine. Great, actually." And I'm putting down my knapsack and walking.

"And you?"

I pull myself onto the island. My legs dangling. Just like I do every night. And he walks over to me. I move my legs to make room for him. He's much taller than I imagined. More real than I expected. And now we're eye to eye. Me on the island and him standing in front of me, leaning forward but not enough to touch. *I've watched your face for so long.* I want to say this, but I don't. I just stare at the collar of his white T-shirt as he brushes some hair off my face. I'm struck by the sincerity of the motion. As if we've known each other for ages. As if we've spent countless nights in basement bars telling each other all there is to tell. Everything told, everything revealed, and it all comes down to a simple gesture. Pushing a stray hair off my face.

"You have a cut."

On my forehead, under the hair he just moved. I must have gotten it that first tumble down the aisle, when Lil slammed the brakes. Now that I know it's there, it stings. "Is it bad?" He assesses the damage. "It'll heal. It's not too deep." He smiles at me. The doctor is M, M is the doctor. It's all blurred.

I allow him to heal me, to dab my forehead with cool

water. And slowly, we begin to relax. I feel my leg skimming against his. His arm brushing against mine. Our bodies melting toward one another in barely perceptible increments, until the stinging subsides. I realize I'm dying of thirst. "Can I have some water?" I ask. There's a glass by his hand. He takes it, crosses to the fridge, and takes out a bottle of water. "Tap water's fine," I say. But he ignores me. And fills the glass. "You don't like tap water."

This is true. "How do you know that?"

He hands me the glass. I sip the water, grateful. His hand resting on my leg now. "I know a lot about you." He looks right at me as he says it. And I look into his eyes, eyes I can't read at this point.

"Like what?"

He moves his mouth, as if he's going to smile. I've seen him do this before. I know he'll stop himself. He won't allow the smile. He catches himself. Bemusement in his eyes. "I know you stole that plasma screen." He flicks his eyes toward my windows. *Do you understand?* That's what he's saying. *Do you get it yet?* And now I smile. Because I do. I understand.

And now I laugh. A laugh I don't remember having. But it's there. I cover my hands with my face. I'm embarrassed. I'm exposed. I'm blushing. "It was Lil's idea. . . ." And now he's laughing. The absurdity of it. We cling to each other, laughing. Until we stop, and we sigh that sigh that comes at the end. And with each moment I feel us growing closer. He takes my hand and looks at me, as if to make sure it's okay. Which it is. And the tone changes. Everything gets smaller.

His voice barely above a whisper, his eyes staring into mine. And he tells me.

"I know that you like to sleep on the counter."

My heart pounding.

"I know you move like a cat."

"I never realized I was so feline." It sounds flip, but I don't mean it that way. I'm just nervous. M knows. He leans in closer, his mouth grazing my ear.

"I know you look beautiful in very little."

All the nights in my underwear. I close my eyes. I can't look at him.

"Parker?"

It's the way he says it that makes me find the words I want to say. "You've been watching my show."

"I have." And now, the trace of a smile across his face. He sighs, still holding my hand, playing with it, turning it around in his own. It strikes me as the most intimate of moments. Him just exploring my hands. It's an odd beginning. But it's ours. And I think it suits us both. "I've been watching you for a long time. I'm sorry."

"For what?"

"For not being able to just talk to you. For barging in on you and dragging an entire film crew into your apartment, just so I could meet you. But I was running out of options."

"And now that you've met me?"

He laughs. "I have no regrets."

I could kiss him, but I don't. I push a hair off his forehead instead. I'm not ready to end this moment. I'm not ready to let go of the anticipation. "Could you show me your view of me?"

"The way I first saw you?"

I nod. "I want to see me from your perspective, because lately I don't think I've been getting the full picture."

TWENTY-NINE

M doesn't bother to turn the lights on. He takes my hand and leads me through his apartment. Big and open, like mine. Only with an eastern view. I spy the faint outline of a sofa near the window, a pile of books, a phone on the floor. There doesn't seem to be much else. From his window, I can't tell which apartment is mine. M puts his arm around me and points. I follow the gaze of his arm until I find it. It's the floor below. I was looking in the wrong direction. And there it is, my lighted room. My set, my life, my show. I realize with stunning clarity that everyone in the alley has seen me in my underwear.

But M was the only one who was really watching.

"I watched as you put up all the colored paper. I'd go to sleep and wake up to check on you, and you'd still be there."

"And before that? Before I started putting up the paper?"

"I'd watch for you. Some nights you were there; others you weren't. But I always looked. And then things got better. You started staying up all night long, sleeping on the window seat. Like you were keeping me company. Some nights I'd stay up all night with you, watching *The Last Emperor*."

I remember that he was reading at the bar. Begley. One of my favorites.

"Did you finish your book?"

"Yes."

"Didn't you love it?"

"I did. How did you know—"

"I saw you reading it at the bar. I was going to say something."

"You should have!"

"I didn't want you to see me like that."

"Didn't want me to see you like what?"

"I don't know. I didn't want you to think that was all I was. A girl who brings you a drink, a hamburger."

"But I never thought that."

His arms are around me now, and I'm resting my head against his chest. "Did you like *Dark Eyes*?"

"Yes, very much. I'd never seen it. Is the girl on the boat the same one who he loved at the beginning?"

"Yeah, it's the same one, only he doesn't realize it until the very end." How fitting, I think. "You can't beat the plasma screen."

"No, you can't."

Down below, we see Stockbroker Guy passed out on his

tacky leather recliner, a new plasma screen on his wall. And his old screen, now mine, is hovering inside the barrage of words that is the Bonnie Cashin graffiti wall. Seeing it from this angle, something about it makes sense to me. Makes sense in a faraway kind of way. Like seeing something through a mist. I see only the outline, nothing more. Yet I know it's there.

"You're writing lyrics, no?"

Am I? I scan the silvery ink. My eyes settle on a grouping scrawled under the screen.

> *The sky is falling*
> *All around the world is spinning*
> *And I'm saving a friend who I can't find*
> *The old man betrays*
> *But we've got letters to save us*
> *Karl Malden can't run now.*
> *That empty suitcase haunting his every move. . . .*

There are more just like it. Scrawled in ink: blue, silver, jet-black. A seemingly endless well of words to play with, to manipulate, to mold, to plot. M is right; the words are lyrics. Simple. Without thought. Just there. Smith's chandelier is spinning. Moved by a light brush of wind, it shimmies and shakes, its rhythm pulling me to the Colorform wall. Pulling me there and then back farther. Much farther.

Until I'm left with an image of my dangling feet. Just like on the island in my kitchen, but it's not the kitchen, and my feet are smaller. Much smaller. I see a battered piano bench. I can place it now. My feet are four, at the most. And Professor Tutshauer, the man with the funny name and the Colonel Klink glasses, is teaching me. His hand, the left one, tapping middle C on our old upright piano. He calls the note "do." Which is how I come to learn it.

"Do, Parker, this is do, but I want you to think of it as the sun, the sun around which everything else orbits, and the sun is warm and yellow and bright." I'm four. I have no idea what he's talking about. But I repeat after him. "Do is yellow."

"Very good, Parker, you have a natural talent for this. Now, tell me, what color do you hear when I play this sound?" He hits the next key. A black one. He calls it "di."

"I hear orange?"

"There is no right answer, Parker; there is only what *you* hear."

"I hear orange!"

"Very good; then remember that."

"Di is orange."

"Forget di, Parker; think only of the color and paint with sound."

Painting with sound, every note its own color. That's what he taught me in those first lessons. My first teacher, talking to me in circles and riddles. But I was too young to dismiss it. Instead, I learned without understanding. And now, here it is in front of me. The colors should match the melodies floating in my head. . . .

"You okay?"

I want to check them, but I'm afraid. Afraid that I'm wrong. "Sure, I'm fine. . . . I'm just looking at the colors. . . ."

"What made you do that?"

They *are* melodies. Songs. Or parts of them at least. "Each color's a different note. . . ."

He points to the graffiti wall. "And those are the lyrics to the songs?"

Exactly. That's what they are.

"Will you play for me?"

I look at Humphrey, perched on his stand by my window. He's known all along what I've been looking for. He just couldn't tell me how to get there. "Soon. I promise." And for once, I mean it.

M leads me to the couch. As we sink into the soft down, the sheer comfort of him astounds me. It's late, and we're both tired. Him more than me. I wrap my arms around him as he buries his head in my neck. Familiar, routine, as if we've done this a thousand times before. Which in many ways we have. I want to sleep, I want to give myself over to it, but I can't stop looking at the colors across the way. I force myself to sing the top line of color, the one I first put up after Lil went missing. The sound is in the color. *Please let me be right, because if I'm wrong, I'm lost. . . .*

I hum the melody on the wall. It takes a moment to remember the sequence of colors and another to realize I've never forgotten them. And so, with feet dangling, I paint with sound. It comes out softly, barely above a whisper, this little song of mine.

And relief washes over me.

It's the same song that came to me the other day! The one I couldn't place. The one I thought I would forget. And all at once, I know what the words will be. I know *exactly* how I will sing it. I know *exactly* how Humphrey will fit in.

I know everything now.

The words on the beam are the lyrics, the colors on the wall the songs. And I would never have seen it if M hadn't found me. All those years were *not* wasted! Everything that happened since has *not* been for naught! Everything I thought I lost is found. All this *and* a million bucks in my knapsack.

M raises his head and looks at me. I think I could spend a long time just looking at him. "It's just like I thought it would be." I've so much to tell him, but for now I keep it simple. Honesty and simplicity.

"You're just like I thought you'd be too." And then he kisses me. One of those soft kisses, the kind you dream about when you haven't kissed anyone for a really long time. Dizzy. I fall into him. Like a warm bath. My M. I feel myself slipping off the boat. Back into the water. And he's coming with me.

★

We wake up early. Wrapped in a fleece blanket he grabbed off the floor at some point during the night. I feel all of him against me, the newness of it, the excitement, still pitting in my stomach. I don't want to move. But he rolls us over and turns to my big window. He laughs as he does it. It's a habit now. Even though I'm here.

"You're hooked. . . ."

"I am."

We both look out his giant window and into mine, to see the next episode of *The Parker Grey Show*. Only Parker's got the episode off, and her old friend Lil is doing a guest spot. And there she is, perched on the island, methodically shaving her legs in the kitchen sink. A pile of books by her side, *Viva Las Vegas* playing on the plasma screen behind her.

"There's Lil."

"Yeah." There really isn't much more to say.

★

Later, I take M to the bodega on Washington Street for an egg sandwich. Inside, the cats race up to him as if he's some long-lost friend. I order the sandwiches and coffee while M grabs a paper. I half expect Caroline to walk through the door, even though I know she won't. M grabs the coffee and the paper and heads out. Thirty seconds later, I grab the warm sand-wiches, wrapped in their starchy white papers, and join him on the stoop. They smell good. I hand him one.

He points to the front-page article about the Toxic Avengers.

"So, this is all your doing, huh?"

I nod. He's impressed with me. Hell, *I'm* impressed with me. He eats his sandwich. Sips on his coffee. We sit like this for a couple of minutes. It's nice. He wipes a piece of some-thing off my upper lip. His hand lingers there for a moment as he looks at me. Taking me in. Then he kisses me. Soft. Sweet.

"I want to ask something of you."

"Anything."

"Why don't you write a few songs for the movie?"

"Your movie?"

He nods. "That song you were singing to yourself last night. I can still hear it in my head. I know exactly where it should go." And he pauses. That little smile of his creeping through. "So . . . ?"

And just like that, I answer him. I say yes. I don't bother with the usual internal litany of self-doubt. I don't question it. Because now I know who I am. I am Parker Grey. Friend, voyeur, blackmailer, thwarter of Eco-Rectifiers, waitress. But beyond all that, I am something else. I'm a musician. I've told myself this a thousand times, but this is the first time I actually believe it. And believing it is less earth shattering than I would have imagined. It's a much smaller moment than I expected. It's very still. Decidedly low key. The only difference now is a distinct sense of entitlement that was never there before. And maybe that's all I was missing in the first place.

"I have to warn you, this movie, it's what they call a labor of love. . . ." His voice pulls me back.

"Which means no one has any money to pay anyone?"

And now he laughs. His eyes shining bright. "Yes, something like that. But I want you to do it. It's fitting, no? You and me together on the screen."

Fitting doesn't begin to describe it.

I was watching him, and he was watching me. It's as if we both met one another from the inside out. And now, somehow we're here—like two old souls—reunited after a litany of karmic failures. If I believed in all that stuff, I'd say M and

I were friends before. I'd say we go way back. But I don't. I only believe in chance and luck and the fact that life makes very little sense. So when something comes along that does, you hang on to it. "I'll do it for free."

"Good, then it's settled."

I like the way he says it. The comfort in the wording.

"I'll see to it that you get something. They're not *that* broke."

"It's okay. I've got plenty of cash." I take a bite of my sandwich, relishing each disgusting, cholesterol-laden bite. "This is *really* great. I'd say it's the best sandwich I've ever had in my entire life."

He looks at me and laughs again. He thinks I'm joking, but I'm not. I mean it with all my heart. It's the best sandwich, the best breakfast, the best start to a day, the best moment. . . . I lean my head on his shoulder and feel the warm sun hitting the side of my face. M puts his arm around me and rubs his hand along my back, absentminded, as if we've sat on this stoop a thousand times before. It's all very matter-of-fact.

Which is exactly why it feels so perfect.

If this were still my show, this is where the camera would leave us. It would pan up to the sky and fly out over the skyline. The city would gleam in the distance, a symbol of the hope that this new day brings. But this isn't a show; this is just my life. And I'm staying right here, my feet planted firmly on the ground beneath me. One of the kittens has come down on the stoop and is playing with my shoelace. I pull my hair off my face, feel the air on my skin. There's a song swirling around my head that I've never heard before. I hum it to myself while M reads all about my Eco-Rectifiers in the paper.

Leaning against him, I feel the faint rise and fall of his body as he breathes.